*The Fox and the Dragons*
A Future History Novel
Sequel to *Come See the Light*
By
Norman Luce
©Norman Luce February 7, 2025
www.normanluce-writer.com
Cover art by Rebeccacovers

Stand with Ukraine Against Tyranny

## Table of Contents

Forward - 3
Authors Note - p.5
Events Leading up to This Story - p.7
Quote - p.13
Prelude - p.15
1: Too Many Surprises - p.33
2: Uncertain Rescue - p.51
3: Uninvited Guests - p.67
4: Coffee Chat - p.79
5: Fangs of Fury - p.89
6: Guarding Kali - p.97
7: To Know You More - p.107
8: No Hard Feelings - p.119
9: Dear Leader - p.125
10: Into the Breach - p.137
11: Reunions - p.157
12: Brooke - p.177
13: Come Home - p.199
14: You Seem Familiar - p.209
15: Chance Encounters - p.217
16: Change in Plans - p.237
17: A Cold War - p.245
18: Forged in Fire - p.261
19: The Belly of the Beast - p.269
20: Land of the Blind - p.279
21: For Whom the Bell Tolls - p.285
22: Her Comes a Walking Fury - p.299
23: Getting Better - p.309
Epilogue - p.317
Appendix - p.325

# Forward

by
James Luce
Author of
*The Mount of Megiddo*

*The Fox and the Dragons* is both a self-contained future history novel and an illuminating sequel to *Come See the Light*, the first of a planned trilogy. This second novel provides the reader with a moving picture, a portrait in words, a cascade of relatable characters and exciting adventures that unfold several decades hence, all emanating from events that happen just a few years from now, thus and uniquely a distant future history of our immediate future history.

The author, Norman Luce, has conjured a plausible scenario wherein climate change, global conflicts, global pandemics, artificial intelligence, social media, income disparity, and overpopulation have all been completely washed away by The Wave…one button pushed by one scientist, Samuel Clarke, Ph.D., who invented something bizarre by mistake.

In spite of Humanity's fumbling failure to take effective action against the intractable scourges of modern times, one scientist's transformative thumb brings all of civilization back to an earlier, but still troubled, reality. A reality that's as old as history itself, where love and compassion do battle with hatred and violence, where science clashes with magic, and loyalty transforms into treachery without warning.

In this novel, you will be transported by thoughtful, sometimes startling word choices coupled with an engaging narrative and salutary dashes of levity into the totally rearranged world of the descendants of the survivors of Dr. Clarke's scientific fiddling. Here you will discover how flexible and yet also how stubborn we human beings and our cultures can be, all without having to move an inch from your favorite chair, couch, or beach blanket.

# Authors note and Dedication

Before you begin reading this story, I encourage you to please take a quick listen to the song "Crossing the Bar" as performed by The Longest Johns. I promise it will play a significant role in the end.

If you are interested in reading the first book, *Come See the Light*, I encourage you to track down and read the <u>Second Edition</u>. It features improved formatting and editing for a much better reading experience.

For my family, my friends, and everyone who has been a light in my life.

# Events Leading up to This Story
## Plot Summery
## of
## *Come See The Light*

In the year 2037, a scientist named Dr. Issac Clarke invents a device dubbed The Wave: a technology with the capability to manipulate the laws of electrophysics, granting The Machine's user the power to eliminate all non-biological electricity, nullifying the use of any other electricity-based technology worldwide, including computers, mobile phones, most vehicles, etc. After the world finds itself on the brink of nuclear war, Dr. Clarke decides that the best course for Humanity's survival is to activate The Wave and remove power from the world until Humanity can once again prove itself worthy of power.

This decision was protested by his partner and friend, Professor Mae Douglass, who pleaded with Dr. Clarke to accept their fate and let the world go with its choice, however misguided. But Dr. Clarke was too stubborn and shut Professor Douglass out, resolute in his decision to strip the world of its power, knowing full well the many disasters and casualties his actions would cause, but secure in maintaining a better chance for Humanity's future.

Cutting to 47 years later (the year 2084), Humanity has reverted to Old-West-style living, surviving without modern technology.

In a small village, Douglass Ranch, in Shasta, CA, we meet our heroine, Maya. A nineteen-year-old third generation survivor with substantial willpower, compassion, skills, and talent aplenty. She lives with her little brother Charlie and her now aged great-aunt, Professor Mae Douglass (known affectionately as Dougie). Maya is very protective of her family and very mature for her age, characteristics brought on by the unfortunate death of her mother as a teenager, causing Maya to grow up sooner than most so she could take care of her little brother.

After Dougie suffers a near-fatal heart attack, she informs Maya, in secret, of her involvement with The Wave and pleads for Maya to take on a journey north to The

Machine. The purpose of this journey was to grant the next generation the power to decide where Humanity might go from here: is Humanity ready to have power restored, or can it survive well enough, if not better, without it? Although Maya was angry at her great-aunt for only now sharing her secret, Maya reluctantly agreed to the journey out of respect for Dougie.

Within the first few days of her quest, Maya met her soon to be best friend and companion, Inari the Fox. The vixen displayed many unusual behaviors on their journey, showcasing an advanced understanding of her surroundings, comprehensive language abilities (understanding human speech without speaking it herself), and a remarkably strong sense of empathy and playfulness, especially toward children. Inari's most prominent physical feature was her dual-colored eyes: one was brown, and the other was blue. Maya and Inari's friendship begins when Inari saves Maya's life from a would-be killer in the woods.

The first significant stop on Maya's and Inari's journey was to The Trade Post: a bustling village in Hilt, CA, protected by a massive gate and wooden wall surrounding the entire village. Here, Maya met Kali, the absolute leader of The Trade Post. During Maya's short stay, she and Kali got to know each other better. Kali revealed to Maya how astute she was, revealing her knowledge of Maya's great-aunt, implying she might know more than she led on. After some further and uncomfortable conversation, Maya and Inari left The Trade Post to continue their journey north, with Kali and her hunting companions, Kyle and Andy, secretly on their trail.

Maya's and Inari's next stop was Ashland, OR, where they met up with one of Dougie's close friends, Michael, and his little girl, Izzy. Inari instantly liked little Izzy, playing together and enjoying each other's company. Michael revealed to Maya a knowledge of the situation, or at least the version Dougie had told him. Much to Maya's annoyance, Dougie had not been entirely honest with Michael, saying she (Dougie) was regularly traveling north to search for The Machine, choosing to omit her direct involvement with The Wave. Maya begrudgingly maintained her great-aunt's secret, hoping she could eventually make it right. After being gifted with a kinetically-powered ATV dubbed The Beast, Maya and Inari continued their journey north to find The Machine, with Kali and her goons close behind.

Sometime later, Maya and Inari reached Portland, OR, and began their search for the location of The Machine. During their search, Maya and Inari encountered Kali and her goons, Kyle & Andy. After temporarily disabling the goons, Maya confronted Kali, inquiring about her motivations and knowledge. Kali reveals to Maya that she (Kali) is, in fact, Dr. Clarke's granddaughter, and she has been searching for The Machine to take control and get revenge on those who were involved and related (directly or indirectly) in depriving her (Kali) of a real choice in her future.

Upon this revelation, Maya found herself in a knife fight with Kyle, one of Kali's henchmen. Maya won the fight by killing Kyle and making a getaway with Inari. Shortly after, Kali and Andy, her other henchmen, found Kyle's body; they made their way to the last place Maya was seen, which was close enough to the location of The Machine for Kali to recognize her old stomping ground and deduce The

Machine's location. In an effort to guard her newly found secret, Kali shot Andy, presumably killing him, and waited for Maya to appear.

The next day, Maya found The Machine and was presented with the power to decide, based on her experience in the outside world, whether a return to the Days of Power was needed. Kali also made her way inside. After a brief fight, Maya and Inari subdued Kali and offered her exactly what she sought: a choice. Kali could either continue her mission by killing Maya and taking control of The Machine or work in tandem with Maya to determine a better path for everyone. Maya wanted to help Kali in her struggle by offering her this choice, and much to her relief, Kali accepted.

To this day, Maya and Kali have kept the operational secret of The Machine to themselves and have built a mutual partnership based on trust, shared trauma, and friendship.

In this next story, that very friendship will see a trial by fire!

"The best way to avenge yourself
is to not become like the wrongdoer."

-Marcus Aurelius

# Prelude

*Winter, 2086, Early Morning*
*The Trade Post*
*Hilt, CA*

As the cultists advanced toward The Trade Post from the west, Kali could see how unfathomably outnumbered they were; it was enough to distract her from the gentle snow fall lightly covering the land. The scattered light from the morning twilight transformed them into ominous silhouettes, reminiscent of a plague of rats, and it terrified Kali! She knew that the droves of men and women, marching towards her guarded and fortified little piece of the world, brandishing spears, knives, and old-but-functional firearms, were cultists who were both ignorant and brainwashed.

Kali's only hope was that at least some of the firearms weren't loaded and were just for show, as even the most resourceful group couldn't produce sufficient enough ammunition in this day and age. How could anyone create the kind of bullets needed for most modern firearms when there's no way to operate the machinery needed for such a task? The Wave made certain of that ages ago. This thought and others raced through Kali's mind as she contemplated what to do next.

Kali was much changed since her memorable encounter up north some time ago. Though her black hair gained a few streaks of silver and her face a few more wrinkles, her green eyes still shined like shaped emeralds with a lively demeanor, and she still carried herself with remarkable energy and resilience. Her strength, both physical and mental, had grown exponentially since she made her pact with her unlikely friend and sister-in-arms, as it were.

"Kali," cried one of the guards who was outside the gate, making his presence known.

"Get him inside," shouted Kali to the gate operators, "now!"

Instantly, several of the guards attempted to move the massive tree trunk away from the main gate of The Trade Post.

The weight of the trunk was immense and it took a minute before it could be cleared enough to open the equally massive gate. Fortunately, the cultists were far enough away that there was no immediate concern for the guard's safety. But as the gate finally opened and the guard leaped inside, a defining whistle sound followed by an assertive thud struck the guard's back, forcing him to the ground face first. His body remained motionless, no doubt due to the long arrow embedded deep in his back. A red ribbon attached to the end of the arrow flew in the morning wind like a declarative flag, drawing attention to the note held in place.

As the gate operators dragged the guard's body away from the gate, allowing the others to reset the locking mechanism, Kali made her way down toward the fallen defender. She inspected the body, looking for any sign of life, but was disheartened to find none.

"I'm so sorry," she whispered as she closed the guard's eyes.

Her attention was then drawn to the red ribbon holding the note onto the end of the arrow. Reluctantly, she untied the ribbon and removed the rolled note. Upon unraveling it, she saw exactly what she had feared. The image was that of an fiercely-aggressive-Dragon, shaped like the letter "D", with jagged spikes, and a fiery, ominous eye, colored inky black against a blood red background. It was the insignia of the Dreaded Dragons! A dangerous and expanding cult she had only heard about in rumors. They swarm the land like locusts, finding established places to seize, colonizing all places in their path, taking few prisoners, if any.

Kali's heart raced and pounded like a scared rabbit. She knew what had to happen next, and she wasn't looking forward to it.

"Ma'am," said one of the gate operators, "what do we do?"

Kali looked up with a defeated expression. She paused and simply looked at the gate operator before her. Her eyes demanding the utmost attention.

"Light the green torches," she ordered.

The gate operator knew exactly what she was talking about, but still could not comprehend the order. Surely, it couldn't be that disastrous of a situation. They had faced small hordes before and held them off with ease. But Kali knew this was different. How she knew, the gate operator could not tell. In any case, as much as it pained them both to do so, there was clearly no other course of action.

"Right away, ma'am," said the gate operator with an uncertainty in his voice.

The gate operator grabbed the nearest torch he could find, marched straight up the stairs to the edge of the fort's wall, and ran across to the center area in full view of the entire walled village. He soon arrived at a large box wrapped in thick wooden shutters that could only be opened from one side. A pair of complex padlocks secured the shutters. Next to the box stood a fellow guard (a young woman entrusted with the title of flame-keeper), uncertain of how to react to her fellow guard's urgency.

The gate operator removed from his pocket a small key painted green, revealing it to the flame-keeper, who looked visibly baffled.

"Orders from Kali," said the gate operator in response to her unasked question. "We must light them."

The flame-keeper hesitated before carefully retrieving her own green painted key from her pocket.

"Give me the code," ordered the flame-keeper.

"What has come before can never be seen…" said the gate operator.

"…but can be felt in the pages of history," replied the flame-keeper.

The two of them unlocked the shutters simultaneously. Inside the box was a massive pile of kindling almost buried in a strange green colored powder. The gate operator placed his torch inside the kindling pile, setting it ablaze, releasing green smoke into the air that would be visible for miles. As the smoke ascended, the flame-keeper sounded the alarm bell, waking up the rest of the slumbering Trade Post. As the villagers woke from their sleep, they stared out their windows and then ran outside to see what the fuss was all about. When they saw the green smoke, all of their hearts stopped for a moment. They knew what was coming, and they wished it wasn't true.

In moments, the entire village was up and running. People were packing their belongings preparing to leave. Others were gathering their weapons and gear in preparation for the impending assault. Parents grabbed their children and hurried them to the established evacuation point at the far end of the fortified village.

Kali made her way to the top of the gate, meeting up with the head guard. They both observed the swarm approaching, moving steadily and quickly.

"I need to send a raven to her," said Kali. "She needs to know about this."

"That might be problematic," replied the head guard. "If that arrow is any indication of their marksmanship, they'll shoot down any messenger bird we fly."

Kali did her best to hide her frustration. "Any ideas?"

"Just one," replied the head guard, "but it's a little risky. I can't guarantee it'll work."

Kali placed her hand on the head guard's shoulder and looked him deeply in the eyes.

"As long as there's a chance."

Kali and the head guard shared a glance forged in friendship and cemented in trust.

"There is," said the head guard. "If you bring that messenger bird to me, I'll do my best to help it on its way."

The head guard took Kali's hand and held it with as much understanding and kinship as he could muster. Immediately, Kali set forth on her task.

"Keep the green fires burning!" ordered Kali.

"Yes, ma'am," replied the head guard.

As Kali made her way through the streets of The Trade Post, she could see all the other villagers making their preparations: store owners boarding up their shops, food venders packing up and preparing to move, families frantically packing up what they could carry. Meanwhile, others were preparing for battle, ready to defend and protect the rest of the village. Kali was occasionally tempted to stop and help people who were in need, but given the urgency of her task, she did not do so.

Kali quickly made her way to her house located near the center of the village. She sprinted her way to her study, grabbed a small piece of parchment, a pencil, and begin carefully writing a short note.

Meanwhile, there was great pandemonium throughout The Trade Post: guards continuing to feed wood to the green fire, villagers still making their preparations, and the soldiers preparing for what might be the fight of their lives. All the while the looming approach of the Dreaded Dragon cult ominously inched closer by the minute. As the head guard looked on with his telescope, he could see the cultists much clearer. Clad in leather armor shaped like scales, armed with spears & bladed weapons. Further away, he saw what troubled him the most.

It was a huge battering ram seemingly as large as the wooden trunk used to seal the gate, if not larger. There was too good of a chance it was powerful enough to breach the gate. How quickly was impossible to predict.

Mere minutes later, The Trade Post found itself bombarded with airborne danger. Arrows randomly aimed flew overhead, hitting guards and civilians alike. Shouts and chants from the cultists permeated the air like a banshee's shriek. Then came the earth-shattering boom from the battering ram at the gate. It hit with such incredible force it shook the very walls of the fort, causing the guards up top, not shot down by arrows, to loose their balance. If they weren't already aware of their troubling situation, they surely were now.

As the head guard continued to fire back at the cultists and ordered his comrades to stand their ground, Kali returned with a messenger raven, her handwritten note secured around the bird's leg. She handed the raven to the head guard with diligent urgency. The head guard took the bird with utmost care.

"I'll see you at the rendezvous point," said Kali.

"No," replied the head guard, "you won't!"

Kali was taken aback.

"What do you mean?"

The head guard explained the situation to Kali. In order to help the messenger bird evade the cultists arrows, he would have to stay behind and wait for the right moment to release it. In this case, the right moment was just after the cultists breached the gate and began swarming inside The Trade Post, when they would be the most distracted and least likely to be firing anymore arrows skyward. However, this meant that he would have to stay behind to release the bird.

"No," said Kali, "there has to be another way."

"I'm afraid not," replied the head guard. "If this message is as important as I think it is, then this is the only way."

Kali could not accept the thought of her friend sacrificing himself in this way, even if it was for a necessary cause.

"Then I'm not leaving you!"

"You can't stay," replied the head guard. "The villagers will need you. *She* will need you!"

Kali looked into her friends eyes with love and respect. She knew there wasn't any other way, though she so desperately wanted there to be one. After a moment, Kali quickly embraced her friend before retreating to the evacuation party. The head guard stayed at his post and watched as Kali made it safely to the crowd waiting below.

As Kali joined the villagers at the far end of the fort, a pair of them opened a small, almost hidden gate, revealing a deep and wide tunnel that had been built to go on for miles. Kali cast her eye over the villagers and determined they were all ready to follow her. She then instructed the tunnel's architect to lead the villagers.

"Everyone move carefully," she said. "Don't run!"

Kali supervised the crowd as they entered the opening of the tunnel, repeating her instructions to them as they passed.

Meanwhile, the cultists continued their assault on the gate. Each blow with the battering ram hit harder and louder. The gate buckled causing the trunk holding the gate shut to snap and splinter away bit by bit.

The soldiers inside the gate stood their ground with weapons ready. Even though they were grossly outnumbered, they were prepared to defend their families and friends. They may not be able to save the village from the control of the Dreaded Dragons, but the could at least ensure their fellow villagers escape from tyranny and death.

Elsewhere, the head guard remained hidden away from all the commotion, with the messenger raven still in hand. One of the thuds against the main gate echoed all through the room where he was hiding, causing him to suddenly look toward the room's entrance. No one was after him…yet.

As calmly and quickly as possible, the head guard whispered a name to the messenger raven's ear.

"Maya."

Outside, the gate buckled more, the splinters from the locking trunk became larger, and the sounds of the cultists drowned out all others. The guards waited, their war faces primed, their resolve unquestioned!

Suddenly, the gate finally gave way. The locking trunk snapped in half like a toothpick, allowing the cultists to swarm into The Trade Post. The guards open fired at the cultists with everything they had: arrows, spears, old firearms, sharp rocks from slingshots, even Molotov cocktails. Sadly, none of it was enough, and in mere minutes, the cultists had completely overtaken The Trade Post.

Fortunately, Kali and the rest of the villagers had all made it through the tunnel, closing the small gate behind them, before the main gate gave way, and would hopefully make their way to relative safety.

The head guard, realizing it was time, released the messenger raven into the air, along with an entire flock of spare ravens. They ascended into the air like a black cloud, flying in every direction. Some of the cultists saw them and took aim with their bows & arrows. They managed to take down a few, but there were too many to make any real impact on the bird's efforts.

Just as the head guard released the birds, a group of cultists broke into the room where he was hiding. They quickly overpowered him and dragged him outside into the courtyard, forcing him down on his knees.

As the head guard looked through the opened gate, shrouded in flying dust from all the cultists, he could see a figure approaching him. A tall figure with broad shoulders and an assertive stride. The figure wore leather scale-shaped armor like the rest of the cultists, but appeared more elaborate with spikes and jagged edges. As the figure came closer, the head guard could see the figures menacing helmet. It appeared metallic and well worn with what looked like metal ribbons wrapped around the head, with slits revealing where the eyes and mouth might be, and it wobbled a bit as he walked, as if it was a tad too big for his head. When the figure was close enough, he could see that there were no eyes, just empty voids.

When the figure stopped, so did the head guard's heart.

"Where is she?" asked the figure.

"Long gone," replied the head guard, "you'll never find her."

The figure stood in place, staring down at the head guard.

A moment later, the figure drew his sword. It was five feet long with two sharp edges like a classic medieval blade, straight out of the fairy tale books. The figure held the weapon at a ready position, all set to strike.

"Where did she go?" asked the figure.

The head guard looked back with defiance. The figure was not impressed.

"Do you know who she is," asked the figure, "who her grandfather was, and what she's done to me?"

The head guard remained as silent and still as a stone.

"I won't ask you again," warned the figure as he waved the blade closer to the head guard's face.

The head guard closed his eyes and took a deep breath. The figure, becoming impatient, swung his blade with enormous momentum, painting the cold air before him as crimson as wine. The head guard hardly felt anything as his head fell to the ground, shortly followed by the rest of him.

"Find her," commanded the figure to his flock. "Find her now!"

# 1
# Too Many Surprises

```
Two Days Later
Douglass Ranch
Shasta, CA
```

Maya was in deep concentration at her work bench. She was working on a special project that had occupied most of her free time for weeks: she had found an old standing lamp leftover from the Days of Power, a tall and sturdy metal pole with multiple sockets for light bulbs covered by a single tube of matte paper. Maya's idea was to remove the unusable electrical components for the bulbs and replace them with candle lanterns of multiple colors. Ironically, she accomplished this by making use of some old and large lightbulbs that were made to resemble stained glass windows from old cathedrals, carefully removing the glass housing and their filaments, allowing them to fit around the entire candle. The effect would be a rainbow colored light source the likes of which hadn't been seen since before the Wave.

Maya had become the newly appointed leader of her Shasta-based little village, Douglass Ranch, and cared for all of her people. Her great aunt Dougie grew to enjoy retirement, though she still hosted classes and story time events for the children. That is, when the kids weren't spending the day playing with Inari, Maya's fox companion, the village's unofficial mascot, and resident welfare officer. Inari's "magic" of spreading joy and calming tense situations made her a friend to all who met her and gazed upon her unusually expressive dual-colored brown and blue eyes. Even with the attention of all the village, Inari always held a special place in her heart for her best friend, Maya, not to mention Maya's little brother, Charlie.

Maya's long, dark hair accented her smooth face, made even smoother by her partial Thai heritage. Her brown eyes still shone like tiger's eye, and she still towered over many of the teenagers and twenty-somethings in her village. Probably the only thing about her that had changed physically was her build. Since her journey two years ago, she took it upon herself to learn some additional fighting styles. She took on a sensei who knew aikido and a little bit of jiu-jitsu. Her previous background in some judo helped her pick up the new techniques with ease and excitement. She also became more efficient with her knife and had perfected her hidden blade weapons, now having assembled one for each arm. Although she also improved her skills with firearms, she did not acquire any kind of long-term interest in them, except for her gifted silver-colored revolver.

Maya would sometimes found herself deep in thought about her journey. She would reminisce about the friends she made, the places she had seen, and the horrors she had to face. Most of all, she thought about Kali, and the agreement they made regarding The Machine. They had been exchanging letters and bird messages every month, checking in on each other, growing a greater friendship than Maya thought possible. Maya began to worry a little, as Kali's letter was late this month.

Just then, Inari burst into Maya's room, barking and jumping up and down! Maya directed her attention to the little fox instantly, completely disregarding her delicate project on the work bench.

"What is it?" asked Maya. "What's wrong?"

Inari continued to bark and leap into the air. Maya recognized this as a sign that her attention was needed immediately. Without thinking twice, Maya jumped from her work bench and followed Inari down the stairs to the living area of the house. When she arrived, she was met with a startling sight.

"Surprise!" cried at least six people.

Standing before Maya was her great aunt Dougie; her little brother Charlie; her friends Joseph the blacksmith, Michael, and Michael's little girl Izzy; and a few other members of the village. They all presented her with a delicious looking, freshly baked chocolate cake—her favorite—and proceeded to sing happy birthday to her.

Maya was stunned at first, but her shock soon turned into unexpected delight. She looked down at Inari, realizing what she had been up to.

"You little devil, you!"

Inari tilted her head to the side, as if to say, "What? What did I do?"

After everyone finished singing to Maya, little Izzy, Michael's now ten-year-old daughter, made a bee line for Inari, who instantly greeted her with loving licks on her face. Izzy, in turn, patted Inari all over before scratching behind her ears. When Charlie joined in, it was pure joy for Inari.

Maya took the opportunity to catch up with everyone. She first met up with Michael, still looking as lively as ever with his textured, dark skin and trimmed beard. His hair was still in dreadlocks and elegantly tied back, with the blue tips beautifully maintained. Maya still wondered how he could keep that little colorful detail.

"It's so good to see you," said Maya, giving Michael a massive bear hug. "How have you been?"

"Oh, the usual," replied Michael. "Been taking care of the Shakespeare troupe since we wrapped up for this season. Nothing special."

"That's being modest," said Joseph as he nudged his way in the conversation. "This guy was just telling me that he's now in charge of the whole Shakespeare Festival. That's a big deal, if you ask me."

Joseph, resident blacksmith and confidant to Maya, maintained his silly uncle demeanor. His long, chocolate hair was pulled back into an elegant looking ponytail, and his green eyes still had a delightful shine to them.

After everyone enjoyed their cake, Inari encouraged the little ones to play with her outside. Once the kids were out of the room, Michael asked for everyone's attention.

"Okay, everyone," said Michael, "this is a special day, indeed. Back in the Days of Power, people could only enjoy alcohol when they reached the age of majority. Since our mutual friend here has hit that milestone, it calls for something undeniably special!"

Michael then produced an elegant looking bottle of wine from his messenger bag. It was made of dark green glass with no label, wrapped in a fine silk purple scarf.

"This is a delicious merlot grown and bottled by a good friend of mine back in Ashland. Like many things in our lives, it was made with love, making it the perfect treat for today's celebration!"

Everyone in the room, including Maya, cheered Michael on. Sounds of delighted anticipation filled the room as Michael poured everyone a glass. Someone commented that there may not be enough to go around, but Michael put that concern to rest, assuring everyone that he had brought a few more bottles with him.

"Speech," cried the crowd in repeated succession.

Despite her humility and slight embarrassment, Maya took the podium, as it were, and addressed her little circle of friends and family.

"Well," said Maya, "this is a lot to take in!"

The small crowd let out some reassuring laughter.

"Thank you all for this lovely surprise, and a big thank you to Michael for not only making the trip down here but for supplying the liquid goodies."

The crowd cheered Michael as he took a small bow in appreciation. Maya continued her speech.

"Um… I am grateful for all of you. I don't think my life would be anywhere near as interesting or as fulfilling as it is, and will continue to be, were it not for all the love I feel in this room. Thank you all for being in my life, and for sharing all the laughs and tears with me so far."

Maya raised her glass.

"Here's to many more!"

Everyone raised their glasses in a toast before finally taking a sip. Maya was no stranger to alcohol: she had enjoyed a few sips here and there when she was little, and occasionally enjoyed a glass of something or other with dinner when she was a teenager. Though she enjoyed it, she never drank to excess, except for when the occasion called for it. But while that might have been acceptable for an occasion like today, she wasn't planning on losing her cool. Especially with such a special vintage.

The first sip was deliciously smooth. Maya could make out hints of cherry, oak wood, and apple, sitting on her pallet like warm caramel, then finishing with a crisp aftertaste with notes of honey and blackberry jam. This was a wine that could only have been attributed to witchcraft, and she loved every sip, though not as much as she loved the company. They all spent the rest of the day drinking, chatting, laughing, and basking in each other's warm company.

At one point during the festivities, Maya noticed Dougie sneaking away into the library. Not wanting to draw attention, she quietly excused herself from the dining area. She found Dougie sitting in her reading chair, taking deep breaths. Instantly, Maya was worried.

"Are you okay?" asked Maya as she placed her hand on Dougie's shoulder, showing her concern.

"I'm fine, dear," replied Dougie. "It's nothing to worry about."

Maya didn't quite believe her great aunt. Although she had survived a heart attack before, Maya was not optimistic about a second extraordinary recovery. Dougie's health had improved a good deal since that incident, but she was still pushing eighty, as evidenced by her once bright silver hair having now turned dull white. Not to mention her slightly increased difficulty walking around, even with her cane.

"Come on," insisted Maya, "what's going on?"

Dougie let out a sigh of defeat.

"I'm just getting old, my dear. There's nothing concerning about that. Not now, anyway!"

Maya could still sense the troubling feeling that hovered over her great aunt.

"Have you told Michael yet? Is that what's troubling you?"

An uncomfortable silence fell upon the room.

"I could never tell him," replied Dougie with a tremble in her voice, "it would destroy him."

"Him," replied Maya with gentle snap, "or you?"

Dougie didn't like where this conversation was going, so she tried to escape.

"Let's discuss this another time."

Maya wasn't having it.

"No, you need to tell him! This isn't my secret to keep, otherwise I'd have told him myself years ago. He deserves to know, Professor. You can't keep it from him forever!"

Dougie retreated into herself in silent shame. It pained her how right she knew

Maya was in her words. This was her mistake and she alone could fix it.

"You're right. I'll tell him soon. I promise."

Choosing to believe her great aunt, however tentatively, Maya returned to the festivities, followed by Dougie soon after.

As the evening rolled over the horizon, it was time to call it a night. Maya, being the perfect hostess, ensured that everyone had plenty of water before going to bed. Even at her own surprise party, Maya had to take care of everyone. Such was the way of her spirit. Even Inari was doing her part, ensuring that the young ones were safe and abiding by their elders. She may be a playful fox, but just like her best friend Maya, she never missed a beat when it came to taking care of loved ones. Joseph and the other villagers returned to their homes, while Michael got himself situated on the sofa. Charlie and little Izzy were placed in their bunk beds built by Maya—a useful present for Charlie's birthday some months prior.

Before going to bed herself, Maya checked on the project she had been working on before her impromptu celebration. Everything appeared just as they were. Relieved, Maya carefully put away her tools and materials for the night. After a quick cleaning of her work space, she donned her favorite night shirt and climbed into bed. Inari jumped in with Maya and licked her face before heading over to her own bed at the foot of Maya's. With a warm feeling in her heart, and a belly full of delights, Maya lay down on her side and prepared for a good night's sleep.

As the darkness passed and the light of the early dawn peeked over the horizon, Maya was awakened by a strange pattering noise coming from the round window near the foot of her bed. Confused, she raised herself up to see what was happening. It was a messenger raven tapping at the glass with its beak. Inari noticed it as well, though she had seen the birds often enough to not consider them a threat. She then looked over at Maya, seemingly just as confused as her friend. Maya hoped this was Kali's late messenger raven.

Maya hopped out of her bed and approached the window, opening it just enough to extend her arm to the bird offering a perch to stand on. The raven obliged. Maya brought the bird in and immediately went for the note wrapped around the raven's leg. Once she retrieved the note, Maya placed the bird on her work bench. At first, the raven seemed nervous being in the same room as a fox, but Inari did her best to reassure the bird against suspicions of any ill intent by remaining in her bed, resting on her belly and keeping her eyes on her friend.

Maya quickly unrolled the note. It read:

> Maya, not enough time.
> Grave danger. Dreaded
> Dragons are attacking.
> Trade Post not safe.
> Escaping to rendezvous
> point. Please help. THEY
> KNOW!

Maya's heart stopped! The terror of those words rattled her very core! Maya couldn't help herself as she fell into her work chair and a million different thoughts raced through her mind: *What do they know? How could they know? How much do they actually know? Who are they? Where is Kali? Is she really safe? What should I do?* Maya's heart was racing, her breathing rapid, her mind in chaos! She could do nothing for the moment but close her eyes and bury her face in her palms in despair and uncertainty.

In that moment, Inari sensed that her friend was troubled. She jumped from her bed and walked straight toward Maya. She gently rested her head in Maya's lap, making soft humming and gentle whimpering sounds. As the fox stayed in her comforting place, Maya's hand gently found itself on Inari's head, stroking her soft and calming fur. Gradually, Maya's heart rate slowed as did her breathing. After a moment, she opened her eyes, looked at her loving friend, and took a deep breath of relief.

"Thank you, girl."

With her thoughts now collected, Maya looked at the note once again. She recalled Kali's rendezvous point was in the old town of Hornbrook, a little less than eight miles south of The Trade Post. On

Maya's special kinetically-powered ATV, the Beast, she and Inari could be there in a few hours. Although Maya had no clue what lay ahead, or in between, she knew that she had to help Kali above all else.

Later that morning, after the sun had finally risen, Dougie woke from her restful sleep and made her way to the kitchen to put a pot of coffee onto the wood fire stove. She was surprised not to see Maya up and about yet, as she was often the earliest riser.

"Maya?" cried Dougie.

Somewhat confused, Dougie proceeded to pour herself a cup, and then she found a typewritten note on the table. It was from Maya. The note read:

> Dougie, I don't have time to explain just yet, but a friend is in danger because The Trade Post is under attack by the Dreaded Dragon cult and I need to investigate. I will try to return as soon as possible. Do not show this note to anyone outside of the house. Tell the rest of the village I went on a hunting trip. Be ready to move at a moment's notice just

in case. Whatever is happening, I promise to take care of it and protect you all. Someone else may know. You need to tell Michael!

Love,
Maya

Dougie couldn't believe what she had just read. Who else could have known about the Machine? As far as she knew, there was only herself and Maya. In that moment, Dougie knew that she had to protect everyone, but she couldn't do it alone. With Maya gone at the moment, she was going to need help, and there was only one person who could provide it. But it meant doing something she still didn't feel ready for. This moment only proved that there was never a "right time" for anything like this.

Just then, Michael came into the room, a bit blurry eyed. He poured himself some coffee before noticing Dougie sitting at the table.

"Morning," said Michael with a smile.

Dougie just sat there, uncertain of how to answer.

"Hey," said Michael, "you okay?"

Still no response. Michael then also noticed Maya's absence.

"Is Maya all right?" asked Michael.

"She's fine," replied Dougie finally, "I hope."

Michael felt a bit uneven.

"What do you mean?"

Dougie looked Michael deeply in the eyes with the utmost command for his attention.

"Please, sit down."

Michael did as he was asked, despite his trepidation.

Dougie took a deep sip of her coffee before clearing her throat.

"There's something I've needed to tell you about for a long time now."

# 2
# Uncertain Rescue

Maya and Inari swooshed through the old roads as fast as the rare ATV, the Beast, would push them. The Beast had proved to be a consistently reliable vehicle on many occasions. Just before the Wave stripped the world of non-biological electricity, rendering things like car batteries and spark plugs completely useless, there was a short-lived push for alternative transportation. One such technology included the very thing that powered Maya's ATV: kinetic energy. Basically it functions much like a flywheel only much smaller and considerably more advanced. With the turn of a small crank, kinetic energy builds up and can be dispersed to create surprisingly useful velocity. The old internal combustion ATV vehicles can be hard to find, but easy to adapt and maintain, and have proven invaluable to those who have done so.

Maya had gathered her essentials for the trip: knife, revolver, hidden blades, bow and arrows, water, canned goods, camping gear, telescope, and other useful items she could store in her backpack or her many jacket pockets. Inari also had some gear of her own. One of the many innovative projects Maya took on over the past two years was to build a protective and tactical vest for her Fox companion.

Using leftover Kevlar from a few old bulletproof vests found on some excursions, along with some suede and a little bit of ingenuity from Maya and Joseph, Inari was outfitted with a vest that proved to be as useful as Maya's jacket, although maybe not as stylish. The vest was obviously strung together from various materials, as evidenced by one section that once had the word "POLICE" embroidered on the front only to be cut off roughly halfway by a new seam. It had side pockets that were packed with a small emergency med kit, some matches & flint, an old compact emergency blanket, and a small knife with some paracord wrapped around the handle. The vest also featured a top handle for potential rescues to hold onto, allowing Inari to guide them if needed. The vest and its contents held together with custom made leather straps and metal buckles.

As Maya drove down the road, she thought about that fateful day with Kali two years ago, when they both found the Machine, the secret source of the Wave that had eliminated all non-biological electricity half a century prior. She recalled the revelations from that journey: how Kali's grandfather was the very scientist who created and activated the Wave, how Kali was stripped of her very volition and agency for her future, and how life seemed to constantly deny her any kind of real choice, until Maya came into her life.

Through their mutual connection to each other and their shared desire for a better future, Maya gave Kali what she had always been denied, a choice! Kali could either complete her revenge against her grandfather by reversing the effect of The Wave, thereby restoring the world as it was in the Days of Power (not to mention killing Maya in the process to tie up loose ends), or she could work together with Maya and come up with a different plan entirely, built upon a foundation of mutual risk and trust. Much to Maya's relief and gratitude, Kali had chosen the latter.

Maya's thoughts were interrupted by Inari's abrupt barks, warning her of an obstacle in the road, the remains of an old car that had been rolled over by the elements. With swift reflexes, Maya managed to avoid it and steer the Beast back on course. They were still in one piece, albeit a little shaken.

"Sorry, girl," said Maya. "Thanks."

Inari replied with a gentle growl, showing her disapproval of Maya's lack of focus while driving. Maya wouldn't have it.

"Hey, you wanna drive?"

Inari continued to look down the road, as if to provide a better example to her friend. Maya returned her attention to the road as well, partially frustrated but mostly appreciative of Inari's keen attention to her surroundings—a trait that had saved their lives on more than one occasion.

Sometime shortly after, they found themselves passing through Yreka and seeing the dragon statue that played a pivotal role in Maya's previous journey up north. It stood strong and ominous in the morning light, it's glass and metal elements shining like polished mirrors. It was a bright reminder of the first time Inari revealed her sense of empathy, providing calm emotional support in a moment of devastating turmoil. It also told Maya just how much farther she had to travel: she was at least twenty minutes away from Hornbrook and that much closer to getting some much needed answers.

When Maya was just a few miles away from Hornbrook, she went off-road to find a nice vantage point from which she could see the town before heading in. She found a small hill that wasn't as high as she might have liked but it sufficed. Once there, she dismounted the Beast and hiked the rest of the way to the cliff's edge, followed closely by her canine best friend and companion. Upon arriving at the cliff's edge, Maya took out her long range telescope and scouted the area. Like many small towns in Maya's world, it was almost entirely abandoned: left behind once the Wave rendered the area unsustainable, causing its residents to move on to greener pastures, as it were. While it was clear that no one had lived in the town for many years, it was, much to Maya's surprise, populated with people.

It was probably the whole population of The Trade Post—now dislocated refugees. Makeshift camp sites spread around a large area within walking distance from the town. Most of the buildings had fallen from lack of maintenance or natural disasters. What buildings remained appeared to be mostly used for storage. Everyone bundled up for the cold weather, sitting close to their own fires and wrapped up in a wide variety of blankets and parkas.

Maya recognized a few of the folks through her telescope: she saw her favorite food vendor who cooked and served those tasty Mandarin style beef sticks and made special chicken ones for Inari. She saw David, the young administrator who first introduced her to Kali. She saw a few other recognizable people but could see no sign of Kali herself. *Come on, where are you?*

After a few minutes, Maya finally caught a glimpse of Kali making her way through the camp, seemingly making sure everyone was all right, or at least as much as they could be. Maya could see Kali helping one person get a fire started after handing over a spare blanket. *Okay, she's fine.* Relieved,

Maya was putting away her telescope, when she noticed something in the corner of her eye. There was a cloud of dust emanating from the road several miles north. Maya aimed her telescope in that direction to get a better understanding of what it might be.

Through the trees, Maya could make out four or five figures moving toward the encampment. They appeared rough looking and bumpy like raisins, and driving kinetically powered motorcycles, much like the ones Kali and her old hunting party had driven before. Maybe these motorcycles were the same ones, but if so, what were these strangers doing with them? They were still a long way away but they were moving quickly. *They've gotta be at least fifteen or twenty minutes away.* Maya then estimated her own distance from the camp of at least ten minutes, which meant she needed to get going, pronto!

"Come on, girl!" said Maya to her fox companion. "We gotta move!"

The two of them hopped onto the Beast, but when Maya turned the key, nothing happened. *Oh, come on!* The Beast had run low on kinetic energy, likely due to the excessive speed in her mad dash to reach the rendezvous point. Maya quickly opened the power crank for the Beast and started turning it as hard and as fast as she possibly could, trying to build up at least enough kinetic energy to get to the encampment, hopefully before whatever's coming from the north could get there.

Inari stood by and carefully watched, wanting to help in some way but having no earthly means of doing so. The best she could do was to serve as an example of the need for concentration, just as she had done for Maya earlier on the road.

"Come on, come on," exclaimed Maya to the Beast as if a machine could understand speech.

After a few minutes that felt like an eternity, the energy meter read just high enough to probably reach the encampment. Maya turned the key, put the Beast into gear, and whooshed down the road toward the encampment at top speed, hoping there would still be enough time to reach Kali before their unwanted visitors arrived.

While Maya was recharging the ATV, Kali headed back to what had been established as the main hub: an old and large army MASH unit tent with wooden frames and a central pillar holding up the canvas. Next to the pillar was an old folding camp table with numerous maps and documents spread all around. The biggest map was of The Trade Post, marked with possible points of entry both direct and discreet. Her official military advisor, a man named Marcus Goldman, looked over the map and shared his observations of the situation.

Marcus Goldman was a stern yet approachable man with a close eye for details and an abundant amount of loyalty to those he cared about. Well into his late fifties with salt and pepper hair and mustache, Marcus carried himself with confidence and determination, with a sense of duty that outweighed his own sense of self-preservation. His grandmother had been a member of the Coast Guard during the Days of Power, and their motto became the basis for his chosen future: 'So Others May Live.'

"I'd estimate they have a force of at least a hundred strong." reported Marcus. "If we're going to stand a chance against them, we need to at least match that!"

"How many soldiers and capable civilian fighters do we have now?" asked Kali.

"At last count," replied Marcus, "the few soldiers who made it out with us, along with the few civilians who registered as 'able to fight,' no more than two dozen at most."

Kali released a sigh of defeat as she contemplated that data.

"What if we took a stealth approach? Make our way inside undetected, take down the forces within, then drive away the remaining cultists? We could refortify our position and make ourselves better prepared if they come back!"

Kali and Marcus carried on a back and forth for a few minutes before they were interrupted by a scout who barged into the tent.

"Kali," said the scout urgently, "there's something you need to see!"

Kali and Marcus dashed out of the tent, following the scout's lead, to the southern facing part of the camp. There was another soldier already there with a sniper rifle aimed down the path. To the naked eye, there appeared to be a distant cloud of dust flying up into the air caused by a vehicle.

Marcus raised his binoculars and looked down the path.

"Be ready to fire," ordered Marcus.

"Yes sir," replied the sniper as he adjusted his aim.

An uncomfortable silence fell upon the scene.

"Well," said Kali, "what is it?"

Marcus tried to get a better look, but the morning fog hindered his perception. He could make out what looked like a single figure on wheels.

"I can't tell just yet," replied Marcus. "It looks like someone on an ATV."

Kali instantly had a suspicion of who it might be.

"Is it a girl driving?"

Marcus concentrated his vision as best he could.

"I think so."

The sniper could now make out a clear human silhouette through the fog.

"I have a clean shot," said the sniper.

"Hold your fire," ordered Kali. "We only have a handful of bullets for that thing anyway."

The tension stiffened.

"Is she alone?" asked Kali.

"Maybe," replied Marcus as he continued to look through his binoculars.

Kali tried to keep the situation cool until she could confirm for sure that this incoming visitor was who she hoped it would be.

"Wait," said Marcus, "there's someone or something else with her."

Kali's eyes widened with hopeful glee.

"Is it a fox?" asked Kali.

The incoming figure got clearer through the fog as it got closer. Marcus could make out a girl and, just as Kali had inquired about, the head of a fox riding behind the girl in a basket on the back of the ATV.

"Confirmed," said Marcus, "a girl and a fox!"

"Again, confirmed clean shot," said the sniper who now had Maya's head in his crosshairs.

"No," replied Kali, "hold your fire! She's on our side!"

"Yes, ma'am," replied the sniper as he lowered his rifle.

"You know her?" asked Marcus.

"Yes," replied Kali. "She's…She's my friend!"

A moment later, Maya stopped the Beast a good five yards from where Kali and the others were standing. Maya jumped off the Beast and ran toward Kali.

"Maya," exclaimed Kali, "thank goodness, you got my message."

"They're coming!" exclaimed Maya.

Kali was confused.

"Who?"

"From the north. At least five of them. I'm hoping they're friendly."

Kali had a sneaking suspicion that they weren't.

"Scouting party," said Kali. "They must be looking for me."

"But who are they," asked Maya, "and why would they be looking for you?"

Kali wasn't paying attention to Maya in that moment, putting all of her focus onto Marcus.

"We need to use this advantage before they arrive," said Kali to Marcus before redirecting her attention to Maya. "How far away are they?"

Maya was irritated by Kali's nonresponse. She had hastened here on a moment's notice under the impression that Kali was in danger, and now this very same person wasn't answering her questions. Maya wanted answers.

"Why are they looking for you?"

"I'm sorry," replied Kali, "but there's no time to explain just yet. Help me deal with this and I'll tell you everything later. Please!"

Maya still wasn't happy about the lack of explanation of the situation. She knew that something was going on and she hated not knowing what it was. Especially when it came to how someone else apparently knew their secret. Maya's mind raced with various ways to respond, unable to settle on any of them. Sensing her friend's unevenness, Inari rubbed her face against Maya's leg, offering her ever reliable calming presence. Maya took a deep breath, exhaled, and looked Kali calmly in the eyes.

"What can I do?"

# 3
# Uninvited Guests

The five riders made their way toward the encampment with an air of chest-pounding determination, eager to please their leader and prove their worth. In the Days of Power, they might have resembled something akin to a classic, dangerous motorcycle gang. Their crude armor and unnecessarily loud vehicles further pronounced their intimidating bravado. If ever there was an image that would best encapsulate the aggression of the Dreaded Dragons, these five riders would surely believe they were so, despite being only an illusory image.

Having spotted a glimpse of the encampment through the trees, the leader of the pack halted his scouting party about a mile or so away. He immediately drew out of his pack a large telescope and scanned the encampment, looking for any signs of organized resistance.

"What do you see?" asked his second in command.

The leader described what he saw to be nothing unusual: a small number of people going about their business trying to stay warm and organized. From what he could tell, there didn't appear to be anything even resembling an armed defense. Nothing that could stand up against their apparent advantage.

"No sign of any soldiers," said the leader.

"Should we head back and report?" asked one of the other riders.

The pack leader contemplated for a quick moment.

"Since they don't have any defenses to speak of," said the pack leader, "we can handle this ourselves!"

The second in command wasn't as certain as his leader.

"Maybe we should still…"

"Shut up," commanded the pack leader. "We can handle a few peasants. We'll head down there, grab the target, and return to the Reaper as conquering heroes! Let's move!"

The pack leader revved his vehicle with as mighty a roar as his fly wheel could muster, and he rode toward the encampment with his fellow riders reluctantly following.

As The Trade Post's refugees went about their business fighting back against the cold, the riders drove wildly into their encampment. Most of the people hid inside their tents to take at least some semblance of shelter, while others simply stayed in place, seemingly out of fright, unable to move.

The five riders, clad in their ominous & intimidating leather armor, barged their way through the encampment with no mind as to whoever or whatever was in their way, running over fire pits and knocking down tents, all the while laughing and gloating like typical bullies on a rampage. The riders wanted to secure their perceived dominance over the present situation, and as the villagers would soon discover, they weren't afraid to get their hands dirty.

After another minute of the riders circling around and through the encampment, kicking up dust with their bikes and generally wreaking havoc, they finally came to a stop in the center of the encampment. The pack leader dismounted as he unsheathed a large, battle-worn and blood-stained machete from his waist, prompting his fellow riders to also dismount and draw their pistol-sized crossbows, loading them with arrows ready to fire. The pack leader raised his repugnant blade into the air, visually demanding everyone's attention.

"Listen up," said the pack leader. "We're here for Kali Clarke! If she surrenders and comes with us, we might leave you all alone!"

The villagers may have been scared of the unruly riders but they weren't stupid. Although they didn't know why the riders wanted their leader, there was no doubt in their minds that there would never be an end to their disruption and abuse.

One such villager, a woman clad in a shawl covering her head, appeared to let her nerves get the better of her, shaking and mumbling what sounded like fear-induced lamentations and generally appearing to be intimidated by the riders.

Noticing the shaking villager, the pack leader approached her as the other riders kept their crossbows aimed at the ready, ensuring that no one did anything heroic. Though the woman appeared to try to stop shaking, her anxiety apparently mounted as the pack leader drew closer and closer until, finally, the moment he was within arm's reach, he grabbed the woman by the arm and dragged her with him back to his bike. With tremendous force he threw the woman onto her knees and hands, resting his machete on the back of her neck.

"I'm counting to three," he shouted. "If Kali Clarke isn't out here by then, this woman dies!"

The villagers did their best to prepare for what was coming next.

"One!"

An intense silence.

"Two!"

The pack leader raised his blade.

"Thr…"

"Wait!" cried out a muffled voice. "Please, don't hurt her. I'm coming out!"

A moment later, the voice revealed herself. It was Maya! She kept her hands raised as she walked towards the pack leader, stopping about five yards away.

"Who are you?" asked the pack leader.

"I'm Kali Clarke," replied Maya. "I'm the one you want!"

The pack leader seemed less than convinced.

"You're not Kali. You're not of proper age. You're lying!"

An awkward silence fell on the scene.

"You're right," said Maya. "I'm not Kali."

Maya then looked down at the hostage.

"She is!"

Confused and annoyed, the pack leader looked down at the hostage and found himself face to face with the barrel of an old six-shooter. Before he could utter another word, a single shot flew straight through his helmet, knocking him dead onto the ground.

Before the two closest riders could fire their crossbows at Kali, they were struck down by Maya as her two hidden blades, shot out of her sleeves like ninja stars, planting themselves firmly into their necks, severing the larynx. Those extra hours of practicing finally paid off. A little farther away, one of the other riders took aim at Maya, only to be wrestled down to the ground by Inari, sinking her teeth into the rider's groin and instantaneously disabling him.

Simultaneously, many of the seemingly innocent looking villagers revealed themselves as the village soldiers, including Marcus. They were armed with blades, spears, bows, arrows, and a few functioning handguns. They all readied themselves against the last rider as he stood still, frantically trying to decide where to aim his crossbow.

As he looked down at his fallen comrades and the armed soldiers closed in, he decided to accept his defeat. The rider hopped back onto his bike and swirled around to drive off in the other direction. He didn't even get ten feet before he was shot down by the sniper, falling off his bike, unable to do anything but watch his ride drive itself away without him before eventually toppling over.

Maya went straight over to Kali.

"You all right?"

Kali holstered her six shooter.

"Never better!"

The two women made their way over to the rider dragged down by Inari. She had successfully subdued the rider by pressing her jaws against the rider's jugular, completely disabling the would-be attacker.

"Dang, that hurts, don't it?" quipped Maya as she quickly tied the rider's hands together with some paracord.

A moment later, Marcus and the other "undercover" soldiers arrived on the scene. After assessing the situation, Marcus turned his attention over to Maya.

"Impressive," he said with a genuine smile of approval.

Once Maya finished wrapping up the rider's hands, she stood up, drew her revolver, and took aim at the fallen rider.

"You can move away now, girl," said Maya to her fox companion, who stepped away as instructed.

Kali ordered Marcus and the sniper to escort their prisoner to the storage building and prep him for interrogation. Maya kept her revolver trained on the rider until he was firmly in the soldiers' grip. Feeling reassured, she holstered her weapon.

Kali gave Maya a congratulatory pat on the shoulder.

"You haven't lost a beat," said Kali.

"How did you know the rider would grab you?" asked Maya genuinely curious.

"I didn't," replied Kali, "but I made sure he noticed me the most."

Maya smiled in baffled amazement.

"You never cease to amaze me!"

The two women exchanged a tender hug, happy in their reunion and comforted by each other's well being. Suddenly Inari was rubbing her muzzle against Kali's leg, showing her affection and gratitude as well. Kali bent down and offered her hand to Inari. After a few careful sniffs, Inari licked Kali's palm before moving on to her face. Kali returned the affection with gentle pats on her soft fur. Maya smiled at the scene before her just long enough to appreciate it before returning to what was of more immediate concern.

"You promised me an explanation," said Maya.

"Yes," replied Kali, "I did."

# 4
# Coffee Chat

Maya settled herself inside Kali's quarters: a large canvas yurt roughly twelve feet in diameter held up by a wooden frame with a large center pole. On one end was Kali's sleeping area—a cot with a few quilted blankets—and on the other was a makeshift desk built out of an old door, held up on all four corners by a few cinder blocks. Maya was seated near the center of the yurt in what could be charitably described as the dining area, which consisted of two old chairs and a small round table, apparently lifted from what was likely an old abandoned coffee shop a few blocks away.

Speaking of which, Maya could make out the distinctive scent of a lovely dark roast brewing on the wood fire stove inside Kali's yurt, complete with a pipe for the smoke heading straight out through the top. Kali had put on an old moka pot: a stove top style espresso maker that uses steam pressure from a water tank on the bottom of the pot, pushing the steam upwards through a small container of coffee grounds and into a reservoir on the top. Kali, who was at her desk with Marcus at the moment, kept her ear out for the bubbly sound when the coffee was done.

In the meantime, Maya was enjoying a remarkable sight. Moments earlier, she had removed Inari's gear vest and let her step outside for some exercise. Much to her delight, she saw Inari instantly become a sensation with the children of the encampment, playing tag and fetch and all kinds of games. Maya was pleasantly reminded of how unique Inari really was, how she could so easily put other people, especially children, at ease with her captivating charm and empathy. A true companion and friend in every way.

After only a few minutes on the wood fire stove, the last of the water in the tank began to bubble inside the reservoir. Upon hearing this, Kali excused Marcus from her quarters and escorted him to the door.

"Excuse us, Marcus," said Kali, "but it's now time for girl talk."

"I'll send the messenger raven with our plan details to our team up north," said Marcus as he exited the yurt. "It should arrive well before us."

Kali then made her way to the moka pot on the stove, picked it up by the handle with a thick old rag, and poured herself and Maya two small cups. The pleasant aroma of the coffee permeated throughout the yurt, much to Maya's delight. Kali served the coffee to Maya with a smile.

"Thank you for being there for us today," said Kali.

Maya gently blew along the top of the little cup before taking a careful sip. It was smooth and slightly bitter like unsweetened cocoa with a subtle hint of caramel, just as she liked it.

"I get the feeling you're in a rather tight spot," said Maya.

"Understatement of the year," replied Kali with a defeated sigh. "They drove us out of the Trade Post a few days ago. I had this emergency site prepared in case of an event like this. Oh, by the way, happy belated birthday!"

Kali raised her little coffee cup to Maya, offering a toast. They clinked their cups together and took another sip.

"But exactly who are they?" asked Maya. "You called them the Dreaded Dragons in your note. Are they raiders in costume or something?"

"I don't think 'raider' is exactly the right word for them," replied Kali. "That would imply that they only wanted our goods and supplies. No—these guys are after more."

Kali then went on to explain to Maya just what she knew. The Dreaded Dragons were a dangerous cult: a group of people, typically brainwashed beyond recovery into believing the strangest and most unreal things, often led by evil and clever manipulators seeking a means of control over civilization. In the case of the Dreaded Dragons, they somehow believed that their leader was a supernatural being sent to Earth to restore the world to the Days of Power and that blind loyalty and servitude to the leader would provide just that.

Said leader was the tall figure who murdered Kali's head guard the day of the invasion. Most of the cultists referred to him as "the Reaper." So little was known about this person that even the strongest of skeptics could possibly submit to his outrageous claims. Rumor has it that no one had ever actually seen the Reaper without a helmet, let alone outside of any piece of the armor. According to cult mythology, even gazing upon the Reaper's uncovered face was an offense punishable by death.

"But why haven't I heard about them until now?" asked Maya.

"Not enough people thought they were real," replied Kali. "Most folks who had heard of them claimed they were entirely isolated to one area—the coastal town of Crescent City—and, apparently, hardly stepped outside of that spot. They were believed to have taken over that entire city. Most maps have that place labeled as too dangerous to travel. 'Here there be Dragons,' as they say."

Maya was still deeply upset by all this. She had heard of isolated societies all over the world, and she knew of groups who chose to believe strange and unreasonable things to cope with the new reality, but it still hit her hard to be reminded of such tragic truths. Like most of her peers, she wished she had the capability to help everyone. But the real tragedy we often have to face is that no one can help everyone, especially those who do not want to be helped!

"Your note also said 'they know,'" said Maya. "Exactly *what* do they know?"

"As far as I can tell," replied Kali, "they don't know about you, your home, or about…that place. They do, however, know about me and my family name."

"They know about your grandfather?"

"Somehow, yes, and they likely want me to tell them where the Machine is!"

Maya gasped in quiet fear.

"But how could they know anything about that at all?" asked Maya.

"I don't think they actually *know* anything beyond my relation to the late Dr. Clarke," replied Kali. "They just know I'm related to him, and they must merely *suspect* that I know the location of the Machine."

Maya let out a small sigh of relief, not entirely convinced of Kali's suspicions, considering the lengths the Dreaded Dragons had gone to so far to retrieve Kali.

"But how would they know anything about your grandfather or the Machine in the first place?" asked Maya.

"I'm still trying to figure that out," replied Kali with a baffled look in her eye. "As far as I can tell, there's no one who can connect those dots. No one who's still alive, anyway, other than you and me."

Maya took a moment to absorb this information. She felt that Kali was indeed truthful, but felt there was something amiss in her words, though not in a deceitful way. For the time being, Maya decided to take Kali's statement at face value, but she knew this conversation wasn't completely over just yet. For now, there were more important things to discuss.

"Okay," said Maya, "what about the villagers? They can't stay here for too much longer. Sooner or later those Dreaded Dragons are going to wonder what happened to their scouts."

"I already have a plan for that," replied Kali with a sudden sense of confidence. "I just finished discussing it with Marcus, and it's already in motion."

Kali went on to explain the plan to infiltrate and sabotage the Dreaded Dragons from the inside so they might take back the Trade Post. Some of their soldiers would don the armor taken from the scouting party, disguising themselves and serving as a Trojan horse. They would arrive at The Trade Post in the dead of night carrying what looked like a prisoner tied and wrapped up in a tarp; when in fact, it'd be a few surprises for the Dreaded Dragons. Upon entering the gate, the soldiers would quietly take down the guards inside and then quickly take their positions to avoid suspicion and detection. Once in the clear, a team of others outside but within close proximity to the gate would create a distraction—something big and loud enough to get the attention of most (if not all) the Dreaded Dragons inside. The disguised soldiers would sound the alarm to the other cultists, direct them to the distraction, and then lock them out of the gate, taking them down like fish in a barrel. Afterwards, everyone would make their return, refortify their defenses, and fully reclaim The Trade Post.

"Okay," said Maya with a hint of hesitance, "that sounds possible, but do we know how big of a force we're dealing with?"

"According to Marcus," replied Kali, "they have a force of at least a hundred strong. Which, according to some of our own scouting reports, has been dwindling down over the past few days, likely due to them sending more and more scouting parties all over the area looking for me. There may also be a code phrase we'll need to know to get inside. With luck, we can learn all we need to know from the prisoner you helped us get—after we've… encouraged him to talk."

As audacious as the plan sounded, Maya felt it was simply too reckless. It was clear to Maya that the Dreaded Dragons must know more about Kali than what she suspected if they were willing to send so many parties out to find her like that and risk loosing their advantage over holding The Trade Post. Maya wanted to further press Kali on the issue but resisted the urge to do so, at least for now. One thing she knew for certain was that if the Dreaded Dragons were serious about apprehending her, then Kali needed to stay hidden and far away from The Trade Post until it was absolutely safe to return.

"Okay," said Maya, "let me talk to the prisoner. I'll see what I can get out of him."

"Are you sure?" replied Kali. "I don't doubt your ability, but what makes you think he'll talk to you?"

"Trust me," replied Maya with an air of confidence, "I have my ways!"

# 5
# Fangs of Fury

The prisoner, stripped of his armor, sat alone, securely tied to a chair in the center of the storage room with two guards on either side of the entrance. His foggy breath was accompanied by his harsh shivering from the cold winter air. Although he prided himself as being a tough sort, resolved to remain loyal to the Reaper, nothing could have prepared him for what was ahead.

Suddenly, he could hear voices outside the door: two women talking to the guards. In his fogged state, brought on by the harsh cold, he couldn't quite hear what they were saying, only able to make out a few words like "talk" and "wait here" in what sounded like a slightly garbled meandering. Immediately, Maya entered the room, looking straight into the prisoner's fearful and frustrated eyes with distain and little sympathy.

"Cold?" asked Maya.

The prisoner didn't respond.

"You know, I've had hypothermia once," continued Maya. "It's not at all pleasant! The shivering, difficulty breathing, and don't get me started on the slurred speech part. I sounded like a drunk."

The prisoner kept his face down, refusing to look Maya in the eye.

"Look," continued Maya, "I normally don't like this kind of treatment of others, even to those who threaten or hurt my friends, but you might have something that we need, and I'd appreciate it if you would please give it to us. You'll get a nice warm blanket for cooperating; been keeping it draped near the fire just for you."

Slowly, almost painfully, the prisoner raised his head and gazed straight into Maya's eyes. Maya looked on with anticipation, but without much hope for hearing the response she would prefer.

"I've… got… nothing to say to you," stuttered the prisoner through chattering teeth!

Maya let out a sigh of disappointment followed by a prolonged silence.

"I don't believe you," said Maya. "I think you have at least one thing to say to me: the password for when you return to your group. You must have one. How else can your leader ensure no imposters?"

The prisoner glared at Maya with fire in his eyes like a caged animal ready to pounce.

"Okay," said Maya, "I've been asking you nicely, but my friend won't!"

With a snap of her fingers, Inari entered the room, snarling and baring her teeth as she looked straight at the prisoner, stopped from pouncing only by Maya's outstretched hand signaling her to hold steady. Instantly recognizing the creature, the prisoner suddenly panicked as he did his best to hold his legs together, trying to protect his most sensitive area, still sore from earlier. Inari's growls grew louder and more deliberate, building tension and anticipation.

"This is your last chance," suggested Maya.

The prisoner struggled against the ropes holding him down, all the while begging for relief, desperately clinging to his sense of loyalty to the Reaper.

"Okay!" proclaimed the prisoner. "Okay! I'll talk!"

Maya stepped closer to the prisoner, anticipating what he might have to say.

"What do you want to know," asked the prisoner.

"What is the password for when you return to the Trade Post?"

The prisoner wanted so desperately to remain loyal to The Reaper, but the resonating rumbling of Inari's growls overwhelmed his sense of pride and duty.

Maya placed her hand on the prisoner's left shoulder as if to reassure him.

"It's okay," said Maya. "You can tell me."

The prisoner's eyes seemed to water with tears, not out of fear, but disappointment in himself.

"Someone will ask, 'Who knocks at the gate?' and you respond, 'Malleus Maleficarum.' That's the 'all clear' code."

"Is that the truth?" asked Maya.

"Yes, I swear, that's it!"

Maya contemplated the prisoner's response and demeanor, looking him up and down for any potential signs of dishonesty. After a moment, she turned her attention to her friend.

"Is he telling the truth, Inari?"

The fox penetrated the prisoner's eyes with an unnerving and steady stare. The prisoner could only stare back with painful uncertainty. Then, after what felt like an eternity, Inari cheerfully walked up to the prisoner, who shuddered and twitched in fear of what was about to come as he frantically squeezed his legs together. Only to be bombarded with licks to his face from the fox, followed by cheerful foxy whimpers.

"I'll take that as a yes," said Maya as she watched and laughed in amusement. "Okay, bring it in!"

As if on cue, Kali entered the room with a large blanket, steaming in the cold air, and wrapped it around the shivering prisoner, still being bombarded by kisses from Inari.

"Okay, girl," said Maya, "that's enough."

The Fox ended her unexpected affection and went straight to Maya's side, where she was rewarded with loving pats and commendations from her best friend.

"What did he give you?" asked Kali as she finished wrapping up the prisoner in the fire-heated blanket.

"He gave me the passphrase," replied Maya.

Maya repeated the words provided by the prisoner. Upon hearing them, Kali was struck by disbelief.

"Really?" inquired Kali.

"Yeah," replied Maya, "really. Do you know what it means?"

Kali looked down at the prisoner with more contempt that she had before.

"It's Latin," replied Kali. "It means, 'The Hammer of Witches.'"

Maya remained uninformed after Kali's explanation.

"Well, what does *that* mean," asked Maya.

"It means," replied Kali, "that these guys are far more dangerous and delusional than we might have thought!"

# 6
# Guarding Kali

With their newly discovered intel from the prisoner, Kali, Marcus, and the rest of the soldiers, along with those civilians who were willing and able to fight, prepared for the plan to retake The Trade Post. Kali thought about the implications from the passphrase they extracted from their prisoner; she vividly recalled from one of her many history books the horrors associated with the Hammer of Witches myth.

According to her recollection, The Hammer of Witches was a 15th century religious treatise on sorcery that was secretly embraced by the Roman Catholic Church. The Church used it as a means of seizing control and power over the people, especially women. The treatise was heralded by the Church as a "full-service" instruction manual of sorts proclaiming to contain methods of "identifying" and "punishing" witches, i.e. independent-minded or "uppity" women. The blood-soaked pages of the book contained horrific suggestions, such as hogtying women and tossing them into a deep body of water: if she drowned, she was human and thus innocent of sorcery, but if she instead floated to the surface, she was proclaimed a witch and burned at the stake. Whether innocent or guilty, the end result was identical. These so-called 'witch hunts' were inflicted on the people for over three centuries until voices of reason eventually put them to an end, at least in the US and most of Europe; too bad it only took tens of thousands of such murders before people started asking questions.

    Although Kali had no reason to suspect the passphrase was directed at her specifically, she couldn't help but ponder what she had done in the past to stir such blind hatred from the Dreaded Dragons. Kali may have been a less-than-stellar person in the past, and she never doubted that parts of her history would eventually catch up to her, but she had a challenging time pinpointing just what misdeed it might have been that would come back to haunt her. Kali decided to put these thoughts aside for now as she continued more immediately relevant preparations for the attack.

Marcus and a few soldiers outfitted themselves with the armor from their would-be captors. Some of the pieces needed to be thoroughly cleaned of blood stains, and at least a few pieces, particularly the pack leader's helmet, needed to be repaired or, at the very least, to appear to be intact. After all, it's a bit challenging to pose as a member of the enemy's scouting party with a bullet hole in your helmet. The hope was that the cover of night would hide their makeshift repairs and patch jobs just well enough to pass as intact from a distance, aided further by the recent passing of a new moon. Patching the armor may not have been ideal, but it would have to do.

"Couldn't you have shot this guy in the leg?" joked Marcus as he observed the crude effort to cover the bullet hole in the cultist's helmet.

"Well," replied Kali, "I'll keep that in mind the next time we get abruptly evicted from our home by a group of crazies."

The two of them shared a therapeutic laugh.

Just then, Maya and Inari stepped into the soldiers' tent where they were all preparing for the silent assault.

"Kali," said Maya, "we need to talk."

"Okay," replied Kali. "We've got a while before we need to go."

Maya stepped closer to Kali's ear.

"Privately," whispered Maya.

Concerned, Kali looked into Maya's eyes. She could see that something was brewing in Maya's mind, something that absolutely needed her attention.

"Boys," said Kali, "give us the room!"

Without hesitation, Marcus and the others exited the tent, leaving Maya, Kali, and Inari alone together.

"What's wrong?" asked Kali. "Do you see a problem with the plan?"

"No," replied Maya, "the plan seems fine. But…"

Kali didn't like the sound of that "but" one bit.

"I don't think you should go with them," continued Maya.

A massive silence fell, as if a sixteen ton anvil had just dropped on someone's head and everyone around just stood there staring at the scene, uncertain if they should laugh or cry.

"I'm sorry, what?!" exclaimed Kali.

"You need to let me go in your place," responded Maya.

Kali stood before her friend absolutely baffled. She was simultaneously grateful for her friend's courage and terrified of the potential consequences Maya could face should anything go wrong, goodness forbid! Kali's initial response was to demand that Maya not put herself in such a dangerous position, but she instantly recognized the futility of such a demand. Not only had Maya proved herself capable of handling these kinds of situations many times before, but Kali also knew better than to question her friend's analytical skills, a trait that Kali had come to greatly admire and appreciate.

So Kali responded to Maya's proposal in a better alternative fashion.

"Why?" asked Kali.

"Listen." replied Maya, "these people are after you, like *really* after you! Until we know exactly what it is they want from you, you can't risk yourself getting caught, should the plan fail. You need to stay far away from all of this until we know what we're really dealing with."

Kali let her friend's words sink in. As much as she hated to admit it, Maya was right. But, even so, she couldn't bear the thought of Maya risking her life like this; she didn't feel like she had earned this level of commitment from Maya just yet. She still wanted to do better by Maya before expecting such a task of her. She owed Maya a lot.

"Okay," said Kali. "I understand, but it's still too risky."

"Don't worry," replied Maya. "It'll be all right. Just take good care of Inari until I get back."

Bewilderment struck Kali's face! Inari looked up at Maya in utter befuddlement!

"What?"

"Inari is staying with you while I'm gone," continued Maya. "She'll protect you until I figure this all out."

Kali stood before her friend totally speechless. Meanwhile, Inari made soft whimpering noises, showing her discontent with Maya's plan. Although Inari had grown to trust Kali, and maybe see her as another friend, Maya was still the most important person to her. She could never fathom the idea of leaving Maya's side for anything, especially when she knew how much she and Maya needed each other.

Hearing her vocalized disagreement, Maya bent down to Inari, wrapping her arms around her furry friend as she stroked her head. Inari could only rest her head on Maya's shoulder, gently nudging her face up against her friend's. After a long and warm embrace, Maya held onto Inari's face and looked deeply into her dual-colored eyes.

"Listen, girl," whispered Maya, "I need you to protect Kali like you would me. I won't be gone for long. I'm coming back. I promise! You take good care of her until I do, okay?"

The fox hesitated before nodding her head in agreement. Maya then stood up, patted Inari on the head, and stood still as Inari, somewhat begrudgingly, moved over to Kali's side. The fox sat down and looked up at Maya with a resolute glance.

Kali looked down at Inari, appreciative albeit uncertain, before bringing her attention back to Maya.

"I'll be coming back for her," said Maya. "She'll take care of you while I'm gone. You can always trust her, no matter what!"

Kali looked at Maya with a soaring heart and a few tears of overwhelming gratitude. All she could muster in response to this great gesture was a gentle embrace.

Kali wanted to find the words to make Maya change her mind, to make her reconsider other options, but she knew Maya all too well to think she could talk her friend down from anything.

"I'll take care of her," said Kali. "I promise!"

# 7
# To Know You More

Maya, Marcus, and four soldiers rode north to rendezvous with their scouting party, which had been observing and sending intel back to the camp in Hornbrook. It was at least a good hour before sunset, giving them ample time to arrive and regroup before executing their plan of attack. Maya felt strange not having Inari with her, almost incomplete, but she knew it was for the best, at least for now. Her resolve to help her friend in need, along with the prospect of reuniting with her best friend, was more than enough to give her the strength she needed to succeed in this mission. In a flash, Maya found herself reminiscing about her previous journey, and how she couldn't help but giggle at the unexpected parallels.

"Something on your mind?" inquired Marcus who was riding alongside Maya.

"No," responded Maya, "just a little déjà-vu is all."

"We're approaching the last known position of our scouting party," said Marcus. "Once there, we may have to leave the bikes and hike a bit to find them. They should have received the messenger raven by now."

Maya nodded as she kept her eyes on the road. Sure enough, not long after, they reached their rendezvous point and dismounted, making their way off the road and into the unbeaten path. They covered and camouflaged their rides as best they could with nearby branches. Once their vehicles were as hidden as they were going to get, the group began their hopefully short hike to look for their scouts.

They all followed Marcus' lead with Maya staying close behind and the others a few feet away, each one on the lookout for threats. Even though the last report from the scouts mentioned little to no enemy activity outside the perimeter of The Trade Post, Marcus preferred a little caution. They hiked and searched for a good fifteen minutes before taking a short rest in a small clearing.

"Take five," said Marcus.

As the soldiers settled down, Maya took the opportunity to approach Marcus.

"So, how do you know Kali?" inquired Maya.

"Oh, it's kind of a long story," replied Marcus.

"I think we've got some time to spare," quipped Maya.

Marcus gave a gentle and friendly-toned "humph" in response.

"Well, I've been her military advisor for nearly a decade now. She took me in and gave me a shot at a better life, like her mother before her did for so many others."

Maya seemed a bit baffled.

"I don't recall ever seeing you at The Trade Post when I was there before."

"I tend to keep to myself most of the time," responded Marcus. "Not really much of a… socializer, as it were."

"I hear you," replied Maya. "I also appreciate my privacy."

Marcus gave a small smile and a gentle almost inaudible laugh in response.

"What about before?" continued Maya.

"Before?"

"Yeah, before you met Kali."

A sense of discomfort flew across Marcus' face. It was subtle but noticeable enough for Maya to see, causing her to realize there was a nerve she had unintentionally struck. Almost immediately, she started to apologize and retract the inquiry into Marcus' past.

"No," said Marcus, "it's quite alright. It's just not many people have asked me about it before."

Maya felt terrible in that moment, even though she subconsciously wanted to know more about the person she was entrusting with her very life. Although she valued Kali's judgement of character well enough, Maya still had fleeting reservations about Marcus and his capabilities. Sure, he had proved his abilities well enough earlier that day with taking down the riders, but that was only one instance. On any other day, Maya would have greatly preferred to take on this mission either with Inari or someone else she'd already vetted. But, under these circumstances, her present company would have to do, and she was certainly going to determine just how trustworthy he really was.

So Maya did what she knew she had to do.

"I don't mean to make you uncomfortable," said Maya, "but understand that I need to know who I'm going into the fire with."

"And you didn't think to ask these questions before you volunteered to join this mission," retorted Marcus with a stern and inquisitive tone.

"Under any other circumstances, yes," Maya quickly responded, "but time wasn't on our side today, so I'm making up for it, and I'd appreciate a little understanding on your part!"

Marcus' face turned red ever so slightly. Maya could tell something was troubling the man, but as much as she felt uncomfortable poking a sensitive point, she needed answers.

Marcus abruptly stood up to give Maya his full attention.

"Fine," said Marcus. "Here's what you need to know for now: Kali gave me a chance at a better life when I thought I didn't deserve one. She entrusted me with your safety, and I intend to abide by her orders or die trying! Is that enough information for you?"

Maya was taken aback by Marcus' tone, in spite of the fact that she had expected it, and, unpleasant though it was, she had what she needed. A deeper inquiry could be postponed.

"For now," replied Maya.

With that, Marcus continued to lead the search for the scouts.

"Marcus," whispered Maya.

Marcus stopped yet again and begrudgingly turned to face her.

"Thank you," said Maya softly.

Marcus' face carefully transformed from frustrated to unexpectedly appreciative, almost as if he were troubled by his outburst and wanted to apologize. But with their tight time frame at hand, all he could muster was a firm nod before returning his attention to leading the search.

Maya's face turned into a small smile as she continued to follow Marcus' lead.

A few minutes later, they came across a dense thicket of short trees, half obscured by the late daylight and the cold misty air. Marcus raised his arm, signaling the others to halt. Maya placed her hand on her holstered revolver. Her muscle memory made her look down by her side where Inari typically was to gauge her reaction, but was suddenly reminded of, and maybe a bit disheartened by, the fox's absence. Maya quickly reverted her attention to the situation surrounding her, trying her best to read Marcus' behavior.

Then, there came a soft voice from the trees.

"The sea is wine dark…" said the voice.

"…And the sky is bronze," replied Marcus.

Immediately, a group of five soldiers emerged from the trees, their arms outstretched to welcome Marcus and the others. Marcus embraced the soldier who appeared to be the leader: a tall and strong looking fellow, probably in his mid-thirties, with dark skin, brown eyes, and a shaved head. Maya felt the presence of a gentle giant.

"Good to see you're still alive, Delroy," said Marcus.

"Hey, I've always been hard to kill," replied Delroy.

Maya stayed back and observed the situation, uncertain of how to approach.

"And who might this be?" inquired Delroy.

"She's with us," replied Marcus. "This is Maya, Kali's friend. The one with the fox that Kali told us about. We can trust her."

Delroy looked the girl up and down, not in a lustful way—more a "can she handle herself?" curious way.

"I don't see no fox," said Delroy.

"I left her with Kali for her protection," responded Maya.

"Oh, I see," replied Delroy with a laugh. "Didn't want your pet getting all messed up in the trenches with the grunts!"

Maya's eyes flamed up with a soft rage as she carefully approached Delroy, getting up in his space and meaning business.

"First of all," said Maya, "Inari is *not* my pet! Second, if she were here right now and heard you call her that, she'd have your nuts in her jaws!"

Marcus knew he needed to defuse the situation.

"She's not kidding," said Marcus, temporarily getting Delroy's attention. "I've seen that canine in action, and you don't wanna be on her bad side!"

"Third," continued Maya, "she's doing her part to ensure you all get your home back, as am I. So if you feel like having a warm place to sleep after tonight, don't test my patience. Got it!?"

Delroy stood in place, absorbing the situation and reevaluating his stance on this unexpectedly tough girl.

"You've done this sort of thing before, haven't you?" said Delroy with a twinkle in his eye.

Maya said nothing as she maintained her glare at Delroy, awaiting a more direct answer.

"Okay," said Delroy. "My apologies. It's good see you know what you're doing."

Marcus put his hand on Maya's shoulder.

"Are we cool?" asked Marcus.

The fire in Maya's eyes slowly subsided.

"Yeah," responded Maya, "we're cool."

"Cool," said Delroy. "Now let's get down to business!"

Delroy directed the others inside the thicket of trees and toward their camp.

# 8
# No Hard Feelings

An uneasy silence dominated Kali's tent as she observed Inari resting by the door. Although she knew that the fox was likely on self-imposed guard duty, Kali couldn't also help but liken this behavior to that of a dog patiently awaiting the return of their master. But this wasn't like any other experience she'd had before. Sure, Kali knew her way around dogs, but Inari was, well, different! She wasn't really domesticated (not in the traditional sense, at least), she was loyally obedient but intelligently independent at the same time, and she understood people far better than anyone could have thought possible. From what Kali had observed, Inari was on a whole other level than any other sentient being.

"So," said Kali, "you want some water or something?"

Inari didn't respond, maintaining her vigilance near the entrance.

Kali decided to pour some water into a bowl and present it to the fox. Even then, no movement. Not even a quick glance at the bowl of water offered.

"Okay," said Kali, "I'll just leave this here then."

Kali placed the bowl of water on the ground close to Inari, sitting herself down on the ground as well.

*What the hell am I doing? Talking to a fox!? I mean, yeah, Maya does it all the time, but still!*

Kali became a tad frustrated, not at Inari's lack of acknowledgement but at herself for feeling somewhat foolish for trying to talk to the Fox. Partially because of how silly it seemed, despite witnessing Maya successfully do it on several occasions.

"Look," said Kali, "I just want you to know that… What I mean to say is…"

*What is wrong with me?*

Inari let out a soft whimper, as if to quietly convey her own discomfort with the present situation. This set something off in Kali's mind that she wasn't prepared for.

"I'm scared, too, okay?"

Inari suddenly looked over at Kali, giving her full attention. Kali hung her head as she let out her feelings.

"Your best friend is out there putting her life on the line, and here you are stuck with me! The same person who once tried to kill the two of you. The same person who, in my ignorance, wouldn't have hesitated to shoot you down when I had the chance."

Inari kept her dual-colored eyes squarely on Kali's as she spoke.

"And now, here you are, protecting me, *me*, of all people."

Silence unbroken.

"I just wish I knew why. Why she would care for me so much. Why she would have you protect me. Most of all, how you can be so on board with this whole idea and...why am I even asking you? For all I know, I'm just coming across as total gibberish to you, and I'm just losing my mind over this whole goddamn thing!"

Kali then stood up and walked back to her bed, sitting on the edge, comforting herself with a hug, unable to resist the tears.

"I don't know if you hate me or not," said Kali. "I wouldn't blame you if you did. But I don't want either of us to lose her. I hope you can believe that. Because I couldn't bare the thought of having to care for someone who blames me for their best friend's death. I know that nothing has happened yet, but that's what I'm afraid of!"

Overwhelmed by her thoughts, Kali rested on her side as tears of uncertainty rolled down her face. Inari watched as her present charge broke down.

As Kali laid there on her side, arms relaxed and outstretched before her, she suddenly felt warm licks on her hands. Upon opening her eyes, she saw Inari licking her palms. After a few licks, Inari looked Kali straight in the eyes, as if to let her know that she heard and understood Kali's words. Kali just stared back in amazement.

A moment later, Inari stepped back to the entrance, took a couple of sips of water from the bowl, and resumed her position, ever on the alert.

Kali just looked at Inari for a moment, initially uncertain of how to react. Then, after taking a few deep breaths, she relaxed herself, resting on her side once again—this time in delighted and unexpected contentment.

# 9
# Dear Leader

On account of the new moon, the night sky was nearly pitch black, covering the massive landscape around The Trade Post. The guards struggled to see through the veil; their eyes constantly adjusting between the night and the torches placed around the perimeter. Not to mention the thin layer of fog hovering through the cold night air, just thin enough to allow between fifty to a hundred feet of visibility, rendering the guards extra vigilant and increasingly cautious—especially with their numbers dwindled down to fewer than twenty; their leader's insistence on so many scouting parties to find one woman had everyone's morale stirring with concerns.

Speak of the devil, the Reaper, still clad in his heavy armor and helmet, sat inside Kali's former house, lounging in her library, looking over a copy of *Asimov's Guide to the Bible*. He perused the book and observed a few paragraphs here and there before chucking it into the nearby commodious fireplace, along with a few other books he apparently disagreed with. Somewhere among that pile of ashes appeared to be copies of literary treasures such as *Confessions of a Buddhist Atheist* and *The Complete Works of William Shakespeare*. The Reaper sat down in the elegant lounge chair in the center of the library, seemingly frustrated and impatient.

A moment later, one of his followers, Captain Doyle, appeared just outside the entrance to the library. Captain Doyle was the Reaper's right-hand man, and he was rumored to be one of the very few people to have ever seen the Reaper's face and lived. Captain Doyle was a younger man of about thirty. His ginger hair curled close to his scalp like a bird's nest, and his unusually grey eyes twinkled in the candle light, further accenting the freckles along his cheeks and the bridge of his stubby nose. He carried himself with a confident and rigid poise.

"Dear Leader," said Captain Doyle as he removed his helmet before entering the library, "I have news."

The Reaper rested his covered head on his fist as he placed his elbow on the arm rest.

"Report," commanded The Reaper.

"No word yet from any of the scouting parties," said Captain Doyle. "Our efforts to interrogate the few prisoners we secured has proven fruitless."

The Reaper let out a silent but heavily felt sigh.

"How many prisoners do we have left?" asked the Reaper.

"Six, Dear Leader," replied Captain Doyle.

"And how many have we executed to encourage the others to talk so far?"

"Two, Dear Leader."

Captain Doyle had a damn good idea what was coming next, yet, despite his proud loyalty to The Reaper and the cause of the Dreaded Dragons, he wasn't too excited about it.

"Then," said the Reaper, "perhaps three time's the charm!"

Captain Doyle hesitated, mustering up his response.

"Dear Leader," said Captain Doyle, "with all due respect, the executions don't appear to have had any motivational effect on the other prisoners. Might I suggest an alternative?"

The Reaper stood up in an angry flash.

"Are you questioning my judgement?" inquired the Reaper.

Captain Doyle tried his best to conceal his fear.

"No, never," replied Captain Doyle, "I just thought that…"

The Reaper approached Captain Doyle with an intimidating thrust.

"You are not here to think, boy," proclaimed The Reaper. "You're here to carry out my orders! Unless you no longer trust me. You do still trust me, right boy?"

"Of course!" replied Captain Doyle. "Unequivocally!"

"Then do as you're told," commanded the Reaper.

Captain Doyle collected himself as best he could as he fiddled with his armor.

"Yes sir, Dear Leader," said Captain Doyle as he swiftly turned around to leave the library.

"Captain Doyle," said the Reaper in a commanding and earth-shattering tone.

Captain Doyle stopped dead in his tracks, quietly terrified of what might be coming.

"Yes, Dear Leader?" stammered Captain Doyle.

"Remind me again how it is that you trust me so… unequivocally."

With barely concealed hesitation, Captain Doyle carefully removed the leather glove from his left hand and held it up for The Reaper to see, revealing multiple scars on the back of his hand and a missing little finger.

"Ah, yes," said the Reaper, admiring the sight before him as though he were admiring an elegant sculpture. "You are dismissed, Captain. Do not report to me again until you actually have something I want to hear!"

"Yes, Dear Leader," replied Captain Doyle as he quickly put his mutilated hand back into his glove.

With that, Captain Doyle swiftly made his way out of the house and toward The Trade Post Sheriff's Office, presently used by the Dreaded Dragons as a lock-up for their prisoners. Captain Doyle burst inside without any warning, startling both the guard inside and the prisoners, who still couldn't get any real sleep since having been taken by their oppressors.

The guard had snapped to attention.

"Captain, sir," said the guard.

"Take the prisoners out to the courtyard immediately," ordered Captain Doyle.

The prisoners huddled together in horror, knowing all too well what that might mean. One prisoner in particular, a little boy, no more than twelve, was the most frightened. The older prisoners put themselves between him and the two Dreaded Dragons, for whatever good that would do.

"Yes sir," replied the guard as he called out the door for more soldiers to help him.

Four brutes of the Dreaded Dragons cult gathered around the cell to assist with the Captain's orders—grabbing the prisoners and dragging them out into the courtyard, beating and screaming at the ones who resisted their authority. At one point, one of the Dreaded Dragons went straight for the young boy, only to be pushed away by one of the adult prisoners. He kept the cultist away for a few seconds before he was grabbed from behind by two other cultists and beaten nearly to death. The young boy could only watch in horror before he, too, was dragged away with the others.

Captain Doyle stood in the center of the courtyard illuminated by a few torches. The prisoners were bundled together and held in place by the Dreaded Dragon brutes, their weapons trained on them.

"You all know why you're out here," said Captain Doyle, "so I'll dispense with the speech tonight. Just tell me what I want to know, and you may all return to your cell—maybe with a few extra rations tonight, in appreciation for your cooperation."

The prisoners all remained silent as stone, even the little boy, frightened and shivering though he was.

A moment later, Captain Doyle displayed his impatience with a cartoonish sigh.

"Bring me the child," ordered Captain Doyle.

The other prisoners scrambled to hide and protect the boy from his fate, but

their efforts were futile against the Dreaded Dragons' strength and numbers.
Immediately, the boy found himself in the harsh grasp of a Dreaded Dragon guard and dragged over to Captain Doyle, who had now unholstered his weapon of choice: an old, fully functional 1911 .45 caliber automatic pistol, complete with a six-inch barrel for increased accuracy and a slightly longer clip for holding additional bullets. Even in the dim torchlight, the gun harshly shined like the blood-stained teeth of a predator.

Captain Doyle pressed the barrel of the gun directly to the boy's temple, held in place by two Dreaded Dragon brutes.

"Last chance, everyone," said Captain Doyle.

The prisoners let out cries begging for mercy and to spare the child, none of which mollified the Captain. He looked down at the boy, who was crying silently, his eyes locked on his fellow prisoners.

"You're a very brave boy," whispered the Captain as he cocked the hammer.

The boy squeezed his eyes shut, bracing for impact!

"Captain," cried out a voice from atop the gate.

Captain Doyle snapped his attention toward the voice.

"What?!" barked the Captain.

"It looks like one of the scouting parties might be approaching the gate," said the voice.

Captain Doyle's expression turned jovial upon hearing this news—so much so that he safetied his weapon and placed it back into the holster as he ran toward the guard post by the gate.

"Sir," cried out one of the brutes watching the prisoners, "what shall we do?"

"Put them back for now," ordered Captain Doyle.

The much relieved, albeit super traumatized, prisoners were all escorted back to their holding cell, while Captain Doyle made his way up the stairs to the gate.

Once at the top, through the light fog, Captain Doyle could see the shapes of the kinetically powered bikes of the scouting party. Eagerly he grabbed a telescope from the guard and peered through it down the path. He could make out what indeed looked like their scouting party, and they had a prisoner wrapped in a tarp. Captain Doyle's eyes brimmed with delight at the prospect of what this likely meant.

"Orders sir," asked the guard at the gate.

"Confirm their entrance code, then bring them inside promptly," ordered the Captain.

"Should we inform Dear Leader?"

"No, not yet. Let's confirm they have the one we're looking for first. Dear Leader will be pleased! I'll be in my chambers; I need a moment of quiet. Retrieve me once you've confirmed their catch."

"Yes, Captain."

With that, Captain Doyle gleefully retreated to his chambers, delighted in his apparent and sudden change in fortune.

# 10
# Into the Breach

Marcus and the rest of his team, clad in their disguises, approached the front gate of The Trade Post as planned. Maya acted the part of the Trojan Horse, draped over the back of the bike, loosely wrapped up in a tarp, posing as the captured Kali. Although Marcus had seen firsthand how well Maya could handle herself, he still felt a tad nervous about her role for the mission—not out of concern for her abilities so much as a fatherly worry. A feeling he was all too familiar with and couldn't bare the possibility of experiencing again. But, like the proud soldier he was, he pressed on, letting his confidence for their success, and in Maya, combat his fears.

The group slowed down as they approached the gate, stopping a good twenty yards away.

"Open the gate," commanded Marcus.

A moment later, the gate guard called out to them.

"Who knocks at the gate?" responded the gate guard.

"Malleus Maleficarum," replied Marcus.

There was an uncomfortable silence in the air. It may have only been less than a few seconds, but it was long enough for Marcus to worry just a little bit. After enough time passed for Marcus to hear his own heartbeat, the gate guard signaled to the ones below, ordering them to open the gate—which they had finally repaired from their invasion—for the returning scouting party. Slowly, the gate opened, and the gate guard motioned them inside.

Marcus and his team made their way through the gate, greeting the two cultists on the inside. Four of them parked their rides off to one side of the gate while Marcus parked his on the other.

"I think we found her," said Marcus "Take a look."

As Marcus distracted the gate guard and the operator with a peek at their "capture", two of the other disguised soldiers nonchalantly made their way up toward the top of the perimeter gate, where they both noted at least two more guards patrolling either side. Using hand signals, the two soldiers separated to take down each of the guards in turn. In the meantime, the other two disguised soldiers remained close by the parked vehicles, keeping an eye on Marcus and waiting for the opportune moment.

Meanwhile, Marcus pretended to struggle with the tarp; biding his time and preparing for what was next.

"Seems pretty quiet tonight," commented Marcus.

"It would be less so if we had more people around," replied the gate guard.

"More scouting parties?" inquired Marcus.

"And then some," replied the operator. "Dear Leader sent out almost our entire army. We're down to just a handful."

"Well, of course the Dear Leader knows what he's doing," said Marcus.

After a moment, Marcus finally unwrapped the tarp, revealing what appeared to be an unconscious woman, hands bound in front and gagged with a cloth. As the gate guard approached the woman with his torch, Marcus carefully made his way toward the operator, who was standing by the gate mechanism. The gate guard held his torch close to the woman, scrutinizing her face.

"Are you sure this is her?" asked the gate guard.

"Positive," replied Marcus. "She had the same kind of weapon on her Dear Leader told us about. Look!"

Marcus pulled out Maya's silver revolver and held it into the air to show to the gate guard and the operator. The moment the gate guard turned his head away from the woman, Maya's eyes snapped open, grabbing the gate guard by the breast plate with one hand and jamming her hidden blade directly into the gate guard's neck. Turns out the ropes weren't holding her hands together but were on each wrist individually, creating the illusion of being bound.

Seeing this, the operator was about to run to help his still struggling comrade, only to be stopped in his tracks by Marcus' fist to his Adam's apple. Marcus then tripped the gate operator onto the ground, swiftly covering the operator's mouth, thus also holding his head down, drawing his knife with the other hand, and then quickly jamming the blade into the operator's jugular.

At the same time, upon seeing Maya making her first move, the two disguised soldiers took down the perimeter guards on the wall with dispatch.

All four of the cultists died within seconds of each other.

As quickly as possible, Maya and Marcus grabbed the bodies and dragged them into the gate operator's station. Once the bodies were out of sight, they waited for the planned signal from their friends. At the same time, the other incognito infiltrators quickly and quietly moved the vehicles further inside the gate, clearing the way and preparing for the next phase. Once the entrance was cleared, they pretended to be guarding the area, all the while awaiting the signal.

"Okay," whispered Marcus, "we're clear. You know your job."

"Right," replied Maya, also in a whisper.

The two of them moved out for the next part of their mission. Marcus quickly grabbed the still-lit torch from the downed gate guard and made his way out the front gate. Meanwhile, Maya formed up with the other two soldiers on the ground and headed for the Sheriff's Office.

Maya and the others stopped just outside the front door of the office and waited. The soldier standing next to Maya, still clad in his disguise, knocked on the door of the office.

"Hey," said the soldier, "could you give me a hand with this?"

A moment later, Maya heard a grumble from inside, and then the guard opened the door and stepped outside toward the live bait.

"What the hell do you need my help for?" asked the guard before being abruptly cut off and taken down by Maya.

The liberating infiltrator quickly made his way inside, removing his helmet and revealing his true self to the prisoners inside.

"Shh," said the soldier. "It's okay. We're getting you out of here. We're gonna take back The Trade Post."

Meanwhile, outside the front gate, Marcus waved the torch around like a flag carrier in a parade. About a hundred yards away, Delroy was watching the front gate through his binoculars. Upon seeing Marcus' signal, Delroy went straight to work with the next part of the plan: lighting some fuses, distancing himself from the sparks.

Marcus continued to wave the torch until he felt it had been long enough to be seen by Delroy. He then extinguished the torch by rubbing it along the dirt path and ran back to his vehicle. He retrieved a large, rusted metal can and carried it back to the outer perimeter of the front gate, where he began dousing the ground all around the front gate. Once Marcus had completely emptied the can of its contents, he tossed it aside and ran back inside the gate to prepare for the next phase.

Then, less than a minute later, came the next signal.

A sudden whoosh in the distance followed a long streak of white light going straight up into the air. The little spark of light hovered in the air for a few seconds before appearing to disappear into the night sky. Until…

BOOM!

A mid-air explosion of circular shaped, multi-colored lights filled the night sky, expanding in size before sizzling away into puffs of smoke. The lights were so bright and the sound so penetrating they could be seen and heard from miles away. Then, as quickly as the first one appeared, another one hit, and another, and another, and another. A whole frenzy of bright rainbow lights and explosions filled the night sky.

Back inside The Trade Post, one of the disguised soldiers pretended to suddenly notice the fireworks.

"We're under attack!" he shouted. "Sound the alarm!"

Another one of the infiltrators rang the alarm bell, alerting all the cultists still inside—including Captain Doyle, who arrived in the courtyard within seconds along with the others—at least twenty in all.

Meanwhile, Maya hid inside the Sheriff's Office with one of her comrades and the now freed prisoners. The window shutters were closed tightly to conceal their presence, causing the lights from the fireworks to shine through the cracks like fireflies.

The little boy, unaware of what was happening, started feeling frightened and was about to get a little noisy with fear.

Maya, noticing this, quietly made her way to the boy, gently wrapping him up in her arms and holding him close, much like how she held her little brother during moments of crisis.

"Shh," gently whispered Maya. "It's okay. Don't be afraid. Those are just pretty lights that are here to help us."

The boy, feeling more assured from Maya's sisterly tone, visibly calmed down, resting his face on Maya's shoulder.

"You're so brave," whispered Maya, "just like my little brother."

Back outside in the court yard, the infiltrators signaled toward the fireworks.

"They're approaching the perimeter," said a disguised soldier.

Captain Doyle drew his sword and called the attention of all who were present.

"Dreaded Dragons," barked Captain Doyle, "are we armed and ready?"

"Always," replied the cultists in unison.

"Then let's make our enemies face our fury!"

"But, Captain," said one of the cultists, "shouldn't we warn Dear Leader?"

Captain Doyle looked his fellow cultist dead in the eyes with blind determination.

"We already have one victory under out belt tonight. Let's grace Dear Leader with another, and show him what our devotion really looks like! We can handle a few scavengers with sticks!"

The cultist seemed a bit confused.

"Wait," said the cultist, "what other victory are you…"

Before the cultist could complete his inquiry, Captain Doyle stared down the path toward the fireworks, pointed his sword, and let out a commanding cry.

"Charge!"

Like a confused swarm of bees, the cultists, lead by Captain Doyle, ran out the front gate prepared to fight what they thought was an oncoming army of soldiers. The one cultist who had questioned the situation earlier soon fell into line with the others. They made their way through the front gate and down the dirt path, continuing the charge a good fifty yards away from the gate toward the fireworks.

It wasn't until that moment that Captain Doyle, along with the rest of the cultists, realized that there was no actual army to fight—just a seemingly endless streak of fireworks. They all stood in place, dazed and confused as they stared up at the pretty display of lights in the sky. It wasn't until Captain Doyle returned his attention to The Trade Post and saw their newly-built gate closing that he realized what was happening.

"Return to the gate!" commanded Captain Doyle.

In a frantic frenzy, the cultists ran back toward the gate, which by now was about halfway closed. In their desperate effort to reach the gate in time, none of them noticed Maya standing above the gate, wielding her bow, loaded with a single fire arrow, aimed squarely at the ground that Marcus had soaked in the strange liquid earlier. Maya held her aim, waiting for the right moment to strike, waiting, waiting, waiting, until…

WHOOSH!

Maya released her fire arrow. As it struck the soaked ground, the immediate area burst into flames, setting a few of the running cultists ablaze and stopping the rest in their tracks.

"Open fire," commanded Maya.

Suddenly, the other soldiers, along with a few of the freed prisoners, popped out from above the gate brandishing bows and arrows and fired on the cultists outside, dropping them like fireflies one by one.

Captain Doyle, realizing his defeat, suddenly chose flight over fight and gestured with his sword away from the flames and into the forest.

"Retreat!" commanded Captain Doyle as he disappeared into the woods.

"But Captain," cried out one of the cultists, "our Dear Leader is still inside. We must save him or die trying!"

Captain Doyle looked at the deadly and dubious situation before him, then looked down at his mutilated hand. His heart was racing, his mind overflowing with thoughts of the punishment he would have to endure for his ambitions, his eyes watering with tired aches and overwhelming fear, until, finally…

Captain Doyle continued running away toward the fireworks, leaving his fellow cultists behind.

"Coward!" cried a cultist before taking an arrow to the back.

In his haste, Captain Doyle didn't look back, keeping his tearful eyes on the road ahead. Even when an arrow embedded itself into his thigh, he didn't stop running. He fought through the pain and kept moving. Loyalty to the Dear Leader be damned!

In a matter of seconds, all of the remaining cultists were dead; The Trade Post had been liberated!

Maya, the soldiers, and the freed prisoners all rejoiced at their success. In that moment, Maya wished she could be celebrating with her best friend but felt even more assured of her eventual reunion with Inari. Until then, she was glad to share the feeling with the present company, including Marcus.

Wait, where was Marcus?

In the midst of all the commotion, she almost forgot about him. She thought that Marcus would meet up with everyone else after he prepped the fire liquid, but he was no where to be seen. Maya then asked one of the soldiers if he had seen Marcus.

"I think I saw him heading toward Kali's house," said the soldier. "Not sure why."

*Why would Marcus go there right now by himself,* Maya thought to herself, *unless… wait!*

Maya bolted in the direction of Kali's house.

During all the commotion, the Reaper remained lounging in Kali's library, seemingly oblivious to the events outside. As he sat in the chair preparing to chuck yet another book into the fireplace, Marcus appeared in the door frame, armed with Maya's revolver, pointed straight at the Reaper's head.

"I know that helmet isn't metal," said Marcus, "so don't move!"

The Reaper said nothing as he glared at Marcus.

"Did you feel anything," said Marcus, "when you took her from me?"

Silence.

"I don't know what you're…" replied the Reaper before being angrily interrupted by Marcus.

"Shut up!"

With his aim still on The Reaper, Marcus walked straight to him, grabbed his helmet, and pulled it off his head. But he was not expecting what he saw, and a jolt of uncertain shock overcame his expression.

"Who the hell are you?"

Before Marcus could get an answer, Maya burst through the front door of the house.

"Marcus," cried Maya.

Marcus reacted to the call, quickly turning his head in that direction. The Reaper used this opportunity to draw a dagger from behind his back and shoved it straight through Marcus' arm, causing Marcus to scream in pain and forcing him to drop the revolver. Before it even reached the floor, the Reaper yanked the blade out of Marcus' arm, grabbed him by the shoulder, forced him around 180 degrees, and pressed the dagger against Marcus' throat.

A split second later, Maya made her way to the library and witnessed the grim scene before her. But as terrible as the situation was, it wasn't nearly as shocking to her as the man holding the dagger to Marcus' neck.

"You!" proclaimed Maya, recognizing the man behind the mask.

Suddenly, the Reaper plunged his dagger straight into Marcus' chest and shoved him straight into Maya, knocking them both off balance and sending them to the floor in a tangled heap. Maya tried to lift Marcus off of herself to face down the Reaper but by then it was too late. The Reaper had already placed himself over Maya, grabbing hold of her jacket and yanking her upwards, slamming his fist into her face. The blow disoriented Maya just enough to slightly blur her vision and create a buzzing noise in her ears, but she could still comprehend what was going on, albeit vastly impeded.

"You spared my life," said the Reaper. "For that, I'll spare yours. Just this once!"

The Reaper released his grip from Maya's jacket, dropping her onto the floor. Unable to move and slowly loosing consciousness, she watched with blurry vision as the Reaper retrieved his helmet before strolling out of the house, unobserved by the soldiers near the gate. The last thing she saw that night was what looked like Marcus picking up the revolver and firing a few shots in the Reaper's general direction before a few of the liberated prisoners came rushing to their aid.

    Then, everything went dark!

# 11
# Reunions

As Maya slowly woke from her deep daze, she could feel the soreness from the bruise on her face. Though her vision was still disturbingly blurry, she could make out bright light from the windows in the space, too bright at first but her eyes soon adjusted. The next thing she felt was the sensation of something warm and soft resting by her side. As she carefully turned her head and her vision became much clearer, what she saw made her heart soar with delight.

It was Inari, asleep at her side. Carefully, Maya raised her hand to stroke her friend's fur, promptly causing the Fox to wake up. Inari was happy beyond measure to see her best friend again, alive and mostly well, and bombarded her face with affectionate licks.

"Ow, ow," said Maya with a laugh. "Not the face, please!"

Inari jumped from the bed onto the floor and leaped into the air, making happy cries and yelps, hopping around like a toddler on Christmas Day. Maya carefully sat up, feeling encouraged by her best friend's display of excitement. Suddenly, Inari jumped back onto the bed and gently rested her head on Maya's shoulder, remembering to aim for the non-injured side of her face. Maya embraced her furry friend with all the love and appreciative warmth she could muster. In that moment, she felt so relieved, so missed, and so loved that she couldn't help but cry a little bit.

"Oh," said Maya, "it's so good to see you, girl!"

Then, a thought came swimming into her still slightly dazed head.

"Wait," said Maya as she released her embrace from Inari to look in her dual-colored eyes, "where's Kali?"

"Right here," said a voice coming from Maya's side.

Maya turned to look and saw Kali standing in the doorway, holding a tall glass of water and a bowl filled with what smelled like oranges. As Kali approached, Maya could see that the bowl was actually filled with a greenish-white gel. Inari took this opportunity to rest her head in Maya's lap, ensuring Maya of her genuine and continued presence.

"Drink this," said Kali, carefully offering the glass to Maya.

Maya accepted the glass from Kali and slowly drank the clear and crisp water, the best kind only offered by The Trade Post. She felt like she hadn't had anything to drink for days. As soon as she gulped the last drop of water, Kali scooped some of the gel into her fingers.

"Hold still," gently asked Kali as she applied the gel to Maya's injured face.

"What's that?" asked Maya.

"Freshly crushed Aloe plant mixed with some fresh orange juice for the vitamin C," replied Kali.

Maya felt a bit better as the cool and refreshing gel lathered over her beaten face.

As Kali tenderly attended to her injury, Maya's mind became clearer, and she now needed some answers.

"What happened?" asked Maya. "Where am I?"

"You're in my bedroom," replied Kali. "After you, Marcus, and the others liberated our home, they sent a messenger raven. We all packed up and returned as quickly as we could."

Maya was a bit baffled.

"How long was I out?" asked Maya.

"According to Marcus," replied Kali, "at least three days. You've been going in and out of consciousness. My doctors treated you as best they could."

*Marcus!* thought Maya to herself. *How could I have not asked about Marcus?*

"Is he okay?" asked Maya.

"Don't worry," replied Kali. "He's fine. He's also incredibly lucky. Apparently the dagger just missed his heart. He's recovering at the infirmary right now."

A strong sense of relief swept across Maya's mind only for her to be suddenly struck by extreme concern yet again.

"Has he told you anything about that night?" asked Maya.

"Not much," replied Kali. "He says it's kind of a blur to him. Although he did mention that he got a look at the Reaper's face. As did you, apparently."

Maya placed a firm grip onto Kali's shoulder, grabbing her attention.

"It was him," said Maya. "It was Andy!"

Kali stared back at Maya, trying and failing to absorb what she'd just heard.

"What?" asked Kali in complete befuddlement.

"One of your old henchmen," replied Maya, "the ones you had with you that day we found the Machine. I saw his face!"

Kali's face morphed into an unusual combination of surprise and disturbance, like witnessing an shocking event you can't look away from.

"No," said Kali, "that can't be true!"

"But it is," insisted Maya. "I saw him, clear as I see you now!"

Kali pulled away from Maya, unable to accept what she'd just heard.

"No, no, that can't be possible," insisted Kali.

"But why not?" asked Maya.

Silence!

"Because…" hesitated Kali, "…because I killed him!"

Maya suddenly became as baffled at her friend.

"Or," continued Kali, "at least, I shot him. I was certain he was dead! I don't know how he could have…"

"Kali," interrupted Maya, demanding her friend's full attention, "what happened that night?"

After taking a few deep breaths, Kali sat down beside Maya, and told her the story.

Kali told her friend about that night two years ago when she was after the Machine, the one that created the Wave responsible for eliminating the world's ability to create non-biological electricity. Her two best hunting partners, Kyle and Andy, joined her on the hunt for Maya and Inari. After the unsuccessful ambush, Maya and the fox escaped and killed Kyle in a knife fight. After finding Kyle's body, Kali instructed Andy to take her to the spot where he last encountered Maya. Then, after realizing the truth, Kali told Maya about shooting Andy and leaving him for dead, not wanting anybody to be aware of what she knew.

Silence.

"What else does Andy know?" asked Maya. "He knew about Dougie the first time I ran into him. Does he know where she is? Does he know where my home is?"

Maya began to have a minor panic attack at the prospect of a madman invading her home and killing the ones she loved most. Inari did her best to ease her best friend's fears, as did Kali.

"No," said Kali in as much of a reassuring tone as possible, "no, please, calm down!"

Maya, remembering her fox friend was still nearby, placed her hand on Inari's head and stroked her soft fur. Kali noticed and remained silent, not wanting to interfere. After a moment, Maya regained more of her composure, giving her attention to Kali.

"I never told him where Dougie was," said Kali. "I never told him the locations of anyone or anything pertaining to my family's past. I only ever mentioned Dougie as part of the connection to my grandfather. That was it! I'm sure of that!"

Maya felt a bit of relief from Kali's words. While she was somewhat disheartened to be reminded of Kali's unfortunate and cold past, she was glad to see that her efforts to reevaluate and do better were still on track. And while she felt she could have easily asked Inari to confirm whether or not her words were true (having proven herself a fine detector of lies in the past), Maya wanted to continue giving Kali the benefit of the doubt. At least for now.

"Fine," said Maya. "Is there anything else I need to know about the past few days?"

"Not really," replied a sudden voice from the doorway, "but I might be able to fill in some gaps."

At the door stood Marcus, alive and well, with his left arm hanging in a makeshift sling. His shoulder and chest were wrapped in bandages with a small blood spot where his treated wound was still healing.

"Marcus," cried Maya in delight.

"I had a feeling you might be awake," said Marcus as he eased his way the room.

Upon noticing Marcus, Inari gently jumped from the bed to greet Marcus with a few quick rubs on his legs before returning to her spot on Maya's bed, as if to acknowledge her appreciation for his well being but also to remind him to be good towards her best friend.

"That fox amazes the hell out of me," commented Marcus.

Maya gave an appreciative smile.

"Anyway," continued Marcus, "I suppose you must have some questions about after the last time you were awake. I'll fill in the blanks for ya."

Marcus went on to explain the events that transpired after Maya lost consciousness that night. Shortly after Maya had blacked out, one of the liberated prisoners revealed herself to be one of The Trade Post's doctors and first gave her attention to Marcus, who was still very much impaled by a large dagger. But Marcus insisted that the doctor take care of Maya first and pulled rank to ensure it. As the doctor and a few others carried Maya to the nearest bedroom, which turned out to be Kali's master suite upstairs, Marcus ordered his men to give chase to the Reaper and pointed them down the general direction he last saw him running.

One soldier stayed behind to attend to Marcus the best he could while two others chased the Reaper. A few minutes later, the soldiers returned to report to Marcus. They had followed the Reaper up the perimeter gate, where they found a rope attached to the other side leading straight down the fort wall and to a parked kinetic bike hidden beneath some underbrush. The soldiers had seen the Reaper having trouble starting his bike. By the time they made their way down the rope to pursue, the Reaper had succeeded in cranking enough energy to escape. The soldiers did their best to stop the Reaper, firing what few arrows they had left from their previous skirmish, unfortunately to no avail.

Shortly thereafter, per Marcus' instructions, Delroy sent a messenger raven to Kali informing her of their victory. Upon receiving word that The Trade Post had been liberated from the Dreaded Dragons, Kali lead her people back to their home. The little boy who had been a prisoner of the Dreaded Dragons was reunited with his parents, and the people promptly began resettling into their homes, while the soldiers began the process of repairing and reinforcing their defenses. They started with hanging the bloodied helmets of the fallen cultists over and around the perimeter fence —a warning to all other would-be-invaders, especially the other scouting parties who had yet to return.

Marcus concluded his recap by mentioning that, despite their best efforts, the Reaper appeared to have escaped their pursuit. All they could report was that he was last seen heading west, most likely returning to his cult compound in Crescent City.

Kali also chimed in and mentioned how Inari, upon entering the newly liberated Trade Post, bolted from Kali's side in search of her best friend, seemingly the moment she likely caught wind of Maya's scent. As Kali chased the fox through the town and then through her house, as soon as Inari found Maya, she jumped into the bed with her and refused to leave Maya's side, barking and growling at anyone who tried to get close to her, except for the doctors whom Inari somehow recognized as the ones who knew what they were doing. The only time Inari ever left Maya's bedside was for an occasional food and water break provided by Kali.

"So, he's still out there," said Maya. "We've got to find him! Bring him down!"

Maya tried to get out of bed and go on a mission, but Inari and the rest of Maya's friends felt differently. They gently helped Maya back into the bed for further rest.

"And we will," said Kali in a gentle tone. "I promise. But not before you're completely recovered. You've already done enough for now, so please!"

"I promise you," said Marcus, "we are doing everything possible to find him."

Maya wanted desperately to get started finding and taking down the Reaper, but her friends all had a valid point: she was in no condition to do much of anything right now, apart from resting and regaining her strength. With her friends there to help her along the way, she knew that she'd be back to full health in no time. She also felt reasonably assured of the safety of her own home as well.

"Okay," said Maya. "I get it."

Maya suddenly felt a massive grumble in her stomach. It was so loud and ominous that it even caused Inari to stand back a bit.

"I think I'll start with something to eat, if I may," joked Maya.

After a round of comforting laughter from her friends, Marcus sent himself downstairs to get Maya some grub. With Marcus out of the room, Maya took the opportunity for just a little more investigating.

"What do you know about Marcus?" asked Maya.

"I'm sorry?" replied Kali.

"How much does he know about you, and you him?"

Kali realized all the implications surrounding that question. After checking the hallway to ensure they weren't likely to be overheard by anyone, Kali returned close to Maya's bedside.

"He knows who my grandfather was, what I've done to protect that secret, and how much you mean to me and why. As for what I know about him, well, I know enough to tell you that you should ask him yourself. It's not my story to tell. But please know this: he will not hesitate to protect either of us."

Maya sat there on the bed, stroking Inari's soft and warm fur, taking in the heavy load of stuff that had just been thrust upon her. Although it was a challenge to process, she was tough enough to handle it, especially with the love and support from her friends.

"Now," said Kali, "please try to get some rest after you eat."

With that, Kali left the room, leaving Maya and Inari alone together. After a moment, Maya finally laid back down onto the soft pillow, comforted by Inari's presence. Inari snuggled up close to Maya, trying her best to help her friend stay warm.

---

Meanwhile, many miles and a few days away from The Trade Post to the west, Captain Doyle sat alone at his lonely camp site, trying his best to treat his leg wound. Even after successfully removing the arrow, he had difficulty controlling the bleeding. He managed to slow down the flow, sure, but he hadn't stopped it entirely. Not to mention the nasty infection he got from the wound that was making it harder to do much of anything. Even his breathing was dangerously impaired. If he didn't get medical help soon, he likely wouldn't need it.

As he sat by his little fire, sulkily scarfing down the rest of his rations, Captain Doyle was suddenly accosted by an approaching voice.

"I thought I would never find you, Captain," said the voice.

Captain Doyle stood up awkwardly, drawing his pistol, desperately trying to locate where the voice was coming from.

"Identify yourself," demanded Captain Doyle.

"Oh, I'm disappointed, Captain," replied the voice. "I thought you of all people would recognize me better than that."

As Captain Doyle turned around to look behind him, he suddenly stood face to face with none other than the Reaper himself, standing before him like an angrily vengeful spirit.

"Oh, Dear Leader, I'm so relieved to see you," said Captain Doyle, failing to hide the trembling in his voice.

The Reaper slowly and deliberately approached Captain Doyle.

"Are you, now?" asked the Reaper. "Because I've been wondering why I'm only seeing you now and not when I should've seen you, oh, about three days ago—when vermin infiltrated my new home and you didn't think to tell me about it!"

Captain Doyle kept his weapon in hand, not aiming directly at the Reaper but getting the strange feeling that he might have to, despite how much he felt that he shouldn't want to.

"Oh, no, Dear Leader," said Captain Doyle, "I was leading the defensive attack when I thought they were invading. I had hoped to approach you with some great news of victory, but by the time I realized what was happening, I was…"

"Too late," interrupted the Reaper, "for any apologies, dear boy!"

The Reaper came within a few feet of Captain Doyle, who was desperately trying to not aim his weapon at his master.

"No, please," begged Captain Doyle. "I would never betray you! I only wanted to…"

Before Captain Doyle could finish his sentence, the Reaper swiped Captain Doyle's weapon out of his hand, swiftly knocked him down onto his back, placed his knee on top of his chest, and wrapped his gloved hands around Captain Doyle's neck, forcing the full weight of his upper body down onto his throat as his hands squeezed the life out of the desperate man.

Captain Doyle tried his best to struggle, kicking his feet and reaching his arms toward The Reaper's helmet, trying to make it all stop. At one point, he successfully ripped off the Reaper's helmet and could now see the face of Dear Leader.

Captain Doyle could feel his life ending as his body struggled for air. The last thing he saw was the Dear Leader's eyes: dark and empty voids filled with nothing but frustration, anger, and maybe just a hint of perverted joy.

Then, Captain Doyle struggled no more.

The Reaper maintained his grip on Captain Doyle's neck even after his life had faded away, making angry grunts and shaking his arms as he squeezed Captain Doyle's head. After several seconds of savage rage, the Reaper finally released his grip, stood up, took a few deep breaths, and peacefully admired what he had just done.

Not long after, the Reaper picked up Captain Doyle's broken body and chucked it into the crackling fire nearby. The Reaper watched as the smoke and flames grew higher toward the early evening sky. After that, he placed his helmet back on his head and strode over to his parked vehicle to continue his journey.

The last part of Captain Doyle's body to burn was his scarred hand.

# 12
# Brooke

After a day of additional rest and plenty of good food, not to mention Inari's special powers of encouragement, Maya felt well enough to get out of bed and move around. Her gait may have been a little wobbly at first but she managed to regain her balance pretty quickly. Inari stayed right by her side the whole time, alert and prepared to break Maya's fall if absolutely necessary. After a few steps down the hallway, Maya found her balance again and was able to walk with relative ease, despite the slight headache.

Maya and Inari slowly made their way downstairs. Kali was there to greet them both, giving Maya a hug and patting Inari on the head.

"How are you feeling?" asked Kali.

"Better," replied Maya. "I could really use a coffee."

"Funny you should say that," replied Kali with a grin.

Kali then made her way to the kitchen and picked up her moka pot from the fire stove. She poured a small cup and offered it to Maya, who relished the sweet aroma and savored every sip.

"Oh, thank you," sighed Maya.

Maya took her time enjoying the delicious concoction so lovingly made by her friend. Then, the moment she finished, there was one thing on her mind.

"Any idea where Marcus is right now?"

Kali pondered for a moment as she poured herself a cup.

"Let's see… I think he's likely at his home. He left the infirmary yesterday, against medical advice. He's stubborn like that sometimes."

Kali provided Maya with some directions to Marcus' home and Maya promptly motioned to head over there, with Inari right by her side as always.

"Is something the matter?" asked Kali.

"No," replied Maya. "I just have a few more questions for him."

Turning around, Maya was just out the door when…

"Oh, before I forget," called Kali, "one of those casual letter carriers delivered a message for you this morning. It's from someone named Michael."

Maya stopped abruptly, one foot on the bottom step. Kali withdrew the sealed letter from her pocket and presented it to her friend. Maya thanked Kali for holding onto it for her, gave her a big bear hug, and politely excused herself, heading straight for Marcus' place.

Maya was eager to know whatever news from home Michael had for her, but she had to clear up something with Marcus first, as it would likely help her decide what to do next. She wondered why Marcus hadn't mentioned the part of the attack plan that involved him taking on the Reaper (Andy) personally. Sure, he had suggested that the Reaper was likely staying at Kali's house while they were in control of The Trade Post, but it seemed strange that he would go there alone. Hell, the chances of the Reaper still being there well after the liberation effort had succeeded seemed dubious at best. Then again, if history of previous dictators and war lords was anything to go by, it somewhat stood to reason that the Reaper would have left the grunt work to his minions while he enjoyed himself in solitude, overly confident in his assured victory.

Whatever the facts were, Maya needed to hear them directly from Marcus before drawing any conclusions. So she put Michael's letter into her pocket for later reading.

A short stroll through town later, Maya and Inari found themselves in front of Marcus' home. As Maya approached the door, she couldn't help but overhear Marcus inside, apparently with a few of his fellow soldiers, discussing additional security plans for The Trade Post. She waited for a break in their conversation to knock on the door. When the opportunity finally presented itself, she was met with a somewhat anticipated response.

"Not now," said Marcus' voice through the door.

Maya wasn't about to take "no" for an answer.

"It's me, Maya. We need to talk, please!"

"Give me an hour, Maya," replied Marcus through the door before continuing his discussion with the soldiers.

Although Maya knew that what Marcus was discussing with his fellow soldiers was important, Maya needed answers sooner rather than an hour later. She didn't have time to wait.

"It's about the Reaper," said Maya.

Maya could hear the voices of the other soldiers muttering to themselves and each other, waiting to see what was going to happen.

"Gentlemen," said Marcus still through the door, "give us the room!"

A moment later, the other soldiers exited the house through the front door. Maya and Inari stood aside as they all left. Each one acknowledged Maya, showing their gratitude for her efforts in taking back their home. Once they had all left, Maya and Inari entered the house, closing the door behind them.

Marcus' home was defiantly marshal in style: highly organized, furniture almost perfectly symmetrical, and antique military memorabilia decorated the walls along with old photos of what Maya presumed were members of Marcus' family. The most noticeable decoration was a painted portrait hanging over the fireplace of a handsome woman dressed in a Coast Guard uniform. Beneath the painting was an elegant plaque carved out of wood, smoothly sanded and treated with oil, which read: "Ut Alii Possunt Vivere."

"So Others May Live," said Marcus, noticing Maya admiring the portrait, "the motto of the Coast Guard back in the Days of Power, before the Wave."

"Did you know her?" asked Maya.

"She was my grandmother," replied Marcus. "This is based on an old photograph I used to have of her. It faded more and more overtime. So I painted this mostly from memory before the photo disappeared entirely."

Maya continued to admire the painting, feeling as though she were getting a better sense of Marcus as a person in the process.

"Sounds like you were pretty close," observed Maya.

"She raised me," replied Marcus.

Maya was happy to have found a bit of common ground with Marcus: having been raised, at least partially, by an older relative.

"You said you needed to talk to me about the Reaper," prompted Marcus.

Maya's full attention went straight back to Marcus.

"Yes," replied Maya, "I do."

Marcus invited Maya to take a seat on his sofa. Before she did, Maya asked if Inari was permitted on the sofa as well, to which Marcus had no objections, and Maya and Inari sat together as honored guests. Marcus took a seat on what appeared to be his reading chair opposite the sofa; the small table alongside the chair was stacked with multiple leather-bound books.

"Okay," said Marcus, "what do you have for me?"

"Actually," replied Maya, "I need something from you!"

Marcus appeared a bit confused.

"What do you mean?"

Maya took a deep breath.

"Kali told me how much you know," said Maya. "If you want me to trust you completely, I need to hear it from you directly. So I want you to tell me just what you know by saying where you stand on all of it."

Marcus knew full well what all that implied, even if he felt somewhat uncomfortable being grilled like this. Although, to be fair, it wasn't really uncalled for, and Marcus knew it. After helping them retake their home, Marcus felt he did at least owe her that much.

"Very well," replied Marcus.

There was a brief silence before Marcus provided was was asked of him.

"I don't condone what Dr. Clarke did all those years ago," said Marcus, "nor do I blame Kali for her grandfather's actions. With that said, I at least understand what brought Dr. Clarke to his choice, and I agree with the reasoning behind the choice Kali made with you. And, like her, I want to be a part of whatever our future becomes, and I will gladly join you and Kali in helping that future become the best that it can be."

Maya took in Marcus' words and meanings, getting the best feeling from them possible. She looked over at Inari and was relieved to see her just as calm as herself, indicating that Inari didn't sense any prevarication or malice in Marcus' words. As challenging as it may have seemed in the moment, Maya felt that Marcus was indeed genuine in his statements.

"Do you find my answers satisfactory?" asked Marcus.

"With regard to Kali and me," responded Maya, "yes, I do. Thank you."

"Okay, then," said Marcus, "now perhaps we could discuss what you…"

"I wasn't finished yet," interrupted Maya.

Marcus let out a sigh of visible frustration.

"Oh, come on, what more do you need to know?"

Maya maintained her calm demeanor, wanting to encourage Marcus to do the same.

"Why didn't you tell me about your plan to confront The Reaper yourself and alone?"

Marcus froze! His mind blanked and the words that had been forming in his throat fell apart. He knew exactly what he would have to tell Maya, but he simply didn't want to. His instinctual reaction was to insist that Maya leave his house. Even so, there was nothing to gain from that course of action. He wanted Maya to trust him, and if that meant sharing some of his scars, then so be it.

"Because," said Marcus, "I wanted justice. But I couldn't have it that night anyway."

Maya seemed baffled.

"Why not?"

"Because," continued Marcus, "that man wasn't the Reaper!"

"And how would you even know that?" said Maya.

After a short beat, Marcus grabbed his left shirt sleeve and raised it, revealing a faded tattoo of the Dreaded Dragons insignia.

Maya stared at the ink on Marcus' arm with a myriad of mixed emotions.

"I told you," continued Marcus, "it's a long story."

Marcus went on to explain his past to Maya in every detail he felt was needed.

Marcus told Maya about his life before coming to The Trade Post. Before earning Kali's trust and becoming her military advisor, Marcus was a member of the Dreaded Dragons. He and his twelve-year-old daughter, Brooke, came to Crescent City searching for a new home. At that time, Marcus was emotionally crippled: he had lost his wife (Brooke's mother) to a gang of raiders who burned down his entire home village. He found himself enamored with the disciplined and organized society offered by the Dreaded Dragons. He even went so far as to almost convince himself of their unreasonable beliefs: that their Dear Leader was somehow a supernatural entity come to deliver humanity's salvation by returning the world to the Days of Power.

Brooke, a precocious young girl, expressed her fears for her dad's well being. She may have been as heartbroken as her father was at the loss of her mother, if not more so, but she still remembered who she was and what her parents stood for. Every chance she had, Brooke would try to reach her true father through the walls he had built around himself, shielding his mind and heart from the pain of his reality. And while Marcus never meant to hurt his little girl in any way, he knew deep down that she was in pain for fear of losing her dad. Even so, his desire to free himself from his own pain through the perceived brotherhood of the Dreaded Dragons outweighed his motivations as a father. At least, at first they did.

No matter how dire things became or how much more challenging it was to reach her dad, Brooke never gave up on him. She always saw her real dad inside, even if he couldn't see himself. And, eventually, Brooke's father would break free from his own prison—sadly, not soon enough.

The Reaper had learned of the girl's dissent from his demands of complete loyalty and set in motion his plan to make an example. One night, without warning, the Reaper, along with a few foot soldiers carrying torches, barged into Marcus' home. The foot soldiers held Brooke in the living room and held Marcus apart in the bedroom. Marcus did his best to defend himself and his daughter, but he was quickly overwhelmed. The Reaper presented Marcus with a choice: Marcus could either prove his unquestionable loyalty to the Reaper and the cause of the Dreaded Dragons by sacrificing his doubting daughter himself, or the Reaper would execute the two of them right then and there, placing their heads on spikes for all the world to see as the consequence of any disobedience.

Marcus recounted how, in that very moment, he realized all too late just how blinded he had become. He had been shaken out of his self-imposed daydream only to wake up to an even worse nightmare. He struggled against the soldiers holding him down, desperately trying to save the one person in the world who truly mattered to him. Through the open bedroom door,

Marcus could see that his baby was hurting, and in danger, and he couldn't do anything about it!

Finally, in desperation, shouting through to the living room, Marcus begged the Reaper for mercy—a futile gesture because since when has anyone as narcissistic as a cult leader ever believed in mercy?

Having had enough of the little girl's cries and impatient from the lack of any proclamations of loyalty to him, the Reaper drew his sword and lifted it for the killing blow.

Marcus recalled how the last thing he saw of his little girl were her eyes, and how they were filled with such sadness and fear and, somehow, love for her father—an expression of love Marcus felt he no longer deserved, but his little girl still left him with, even after her life was abruptly ended by a single swing of the Reaper's blade.

Suddenly, everything turned red! Marcus recalled screaming in anguish as the sight of his lost little girl gave him the strength to break free of the cultists' grip. He then slammed and locked the bedroom door, isolating himself from the Reaper and the two cultists in the living room. Swirling away from the door, Marcus bashed in the faces of the two cultists with bone-shattering force. He then attacked the third cultist, causing him to drop his torch by the window, setting the curtains ablaze. Marcus hardly noticed the flames as he rammed the fourth cultist's head into the wall again, and again, and again, painting the cultist's helmet crimson. As the flames grew higher, two cultist burst through the door from the living room. They were dispatched as quickly and even more brutally than the others.

Suddenly, there was only Marcus, the Reaper, and the fire engulfing the house. The Reaper went straight on toward Marcus with his blood-stained sword held high in preparation for another killing blow, but Marcus ran straight for the Reaper's midsection like a rabid wrestler, knocking the Reaper backwards and through the flaming wall to the outside. Marcus threw the Reaper down onto the the dirt with so much force that the Reaper lost his grip on his sword. Marcus had his daughter's killer pinned down and was about to show him what 'no mercy' really looked like.

Marcus ripped off the Reapers helmet, getting a good look at his true face before slamming it over and over again with his fists. Marcus was prepared to just keep on hitting until the monster beneath him stopped breathing. After only a few blows to the head, Marcus might have succeeded, were it not for the sound of arrows flying around his head and body. Marcus looked off to his side to find another group of cultists who had arrived to investigate the fire and begun shooting arrows at him. Marcus was prepared to ignore the arrows and continue his rage-induced beating, only to be met with a sharp blow from the Reaper solidly into his face, knocking him off to the side.

Marcus rolled over, disoriented but still angry. The Reaper leaped onto his feet and retrieved his helmet before the others got close enough to also see his face. A moment later, Marcus also stood back up. Upon seeing the ominous sight before him—the Reaper still standing and a band of shooters approaching, all silhouetted by the fire—Marcus knew he didn't stand a chance. So he did the only thing he knew was right. He ran!

Marcus made his way toward the old main road, the night enabling him to evade the shooters. Marcus could hear the Reaper's cries, calling him a traitor and swearing to kill him if he ever returned. Marcus ignored all of the commotion as he ran through the night, eventually escaping the city. Even after he reached the outskirts, he kept running.

For the next few days, Marcus kept moving. He had slowed down to a weakened and painful saunter rather than a run. He refused to stop for anything, even when his body begged him to eat or drink something, anything! Marcus just kept moving forward, waiting to die, waiting for his fated punishment for his actions.

Finally, out of total exhaustion, Marcus fell onto the ground on his back, facing the clear sky above, waiting for his last moment to pass.

As Marcus closed his eyes, he kept his remaining thoughts on those wonderful days when he had seen his little girl smile.

When Marcus finally woke up, he thought he had indeed "passed over." as they say. But alas, he was still very much in the world of the living. He had been found by a group of hunters from The Trade Post who carried him back to their home for treatment. Kali introduced him to her home and their way of life, for she could see that he was broken, much like herself, and offered her hand in friendship. After some time, Marcus grew to trust Kali enough with his story, as Kali trusted Marcus with hers.

"…and I've been here ever since," said Marcus, "trying to do better and to honor my daughter's memory."

Maya looked at Marcus with a renewed and deeper appreciation.

"She would have been about your age now," commented Marcus. "I see some of her in you. That resolve, compassion, strength. I think you two would have gotten along very well."

Marcus did his best to ignore the tears in his eyes.

"I'm sorry," whispered Maya. "I didn't mean to make you…"

"Don't worry," said Marcus, gently interrupting. "You have nothing to apologize for."

"Yes, I do," replied Maya.

There was an awkward silence in the room as Marcus waited for Maya to elaborate on her statement. Maya looked at Inari as she stroked her fur, noticed how calm she appeared, and then gave her attention back to Marcus.

"I know all too well," said Maya, "what it feels like to have someone you love taken away from you. I'm sorry I didn't see it before."

"Well," replied Marcus with a grin, "not all of us can wear our hearts on our sleeves."

For a moment, Maya and Marcus sat together in silence, appreciating their better understanding of each other and finding solace in their shared trauma.

Suddenly, Inari sat up and approached Marcus, resting her head on his lap, inviting Marcus to pet her. Marcus looked at Maya, seeking approval.

"She's waiting," said Maya with a smile.

Cautiously, Marcus raised his hand and gently stroked Inari's soft and warm fur. Inari made many happy sounds as Marcus patted her head. Marcus, in turn, smiled the widest smile he ever had in a long time. Inari had once again worked her mysterious magic and made a person in need feel seen, wanted, and loved.

# 13
# Come Home

Maya and Inari walked out of Marcus' home not expecting to feel the ways they did. Maya may have gone in there expecting to confront a potential enemy, having suspected that Marcus might have been in league with the Reaper somehow, but while some of her suspicions had been proven right in part, the rest of his story threw Maya for a loop. She could see through his eyes how genuine and sincere his story was. Even Inari felt the weight of it all, probably what prompted her to offer her special comfort. Maya suddenly remembered an observation made by one of the elders back home: in the Days of Power, Inari would have been called a magnificent therapy animal.

*Wait, home,* thought Maya to herself. *Michael's letter!*

In the midst of all of this, Maya had forgotten about the letter from home. Without a second thought Maya reached into her pocket, took out the letter, broke the seal, and unfolded the paper. The letter read:

Dear Maya,

I hope this letter finds you well and soon. I don't even know if you will be around to receive it but I needed to try. When you told Dougie that you had to help a friend in need, I figured it must have been someone at The Trade Post, so that is where I'm starting.

First, you should know that Dougie has told me everything! Before you presume anything, please know that I am not angry with you. I may be a little disappointed in Dougie, but not you. Dougie made it abundantly clear that it was her secret alone to keep and to share. As far as I am concerned, you did right by everyone involved.

Second, the folks at Douglass Ranch are starting to get a little restless from your absence. Dougie and I are doing all we can to keep the peace, but they need to at least hear from you, to know that you're safe and haven't abandoned them. Either please come home or send over a message.

Third, whatever happens from here on out, I will always consider you a friend. I trust that you will do whatever is right by me, Izzy, and everyone else you care about. I've never had a reason to doubt you, so please don't give me one!

Sincerely,
Michael

Maya's mood shifted instantly from contented to concerned! She immediately started to contemplate the best course of action. She didn't quite trust herself to drive well just yet, so going straight home was out of the question, at least for now. The only viable option was to send a messenger raven. The only question is was there was one available.

Maya ran straight back to Kali's house with Inari close behind. In moments, Maya burst through the front door and searched for Kali, only to find her sitting by the fireplace in the living room. Kali was so surprised that she nearly jumped out of her seat.

"Maya, what's wrong?" asked Kali.

"Home," replied Maya. "I need to send a messenger raven to home. Do you have any to spare?"

Kali showed concern about this sudden need for Maya to reach home.

"What's going on?" asked Kali, "Is everything alright?"

"It's fine," said Maya. "They just need to know I'm okay. I thought I would only be gone for a day or two at most."

Kali let out an ambiguous sigh.

"Well, that might be a problem. We don't have any messenger ravens to spare. The few we had left have already been sent out to some of our neighboring villages, asking for help rebuilding and for reinforcements in case the Dreaded Dragons come back."

Maya's frustrations were starting to get the better of her—not so much to make Inari feel that she needed to intervene, just enough to make her a little extra worried. Maya tried to collect her thoughts.

"Okay," said Maya. "Well, I don't trust myself to drive just yet, so I can't ride the Beast home."

"Alright," said Kali, "tell you what. Why don't I take you and Inari back home? I have a sidecar I can attach to my kinetic bike, and it should be just big enough for the two of you. We'll drive down together, reassure your people of your well being, then we can go from there. I'll also have one of the soldiers drive the Beast down with us for you."

Maya was greatly appreciative of this thoughtful gesture. Even so, there was still one lingering concern floating in Maya's head.

"What about the Reaper?" asked Maya . "He's still out there and he might still try to come after you."

Kali responded with a confident and polite shrug.

"Honey," said Kali, "his army is scattered and he was last scene heading west, likely back to his cult camp to lick his wounds. He'd have to be stupid to try and come after me now."

Maya found a fair amount of logic in Kali's words.

"Okay," said Maya, "but why don't you just send one of your soldiers with me? You can still stay here for your safety."

Kali placed her hand on Maya's shoulder.

"You did so much for me over the past few days. The least I can do is take you home myself. Besides, it'll be a great excuse for me to finally visit your home, see your family."

Maya's concerns were shrinking by the minute.

"What about your people?" asked Maya. "They need you now more than ever."

"Don't worry," responded Kali. "I'll leave Marcus in charge. He's done it before and my people will be fine. We've already got most of our new defenses up and plenty more on the way."

Maya thought about Kali's proposal for a bit. With no other options left, it was arguably the best solution. Maya looked at Inari to try and gauge her reaction to the idea. The fox looked up at Maya with a look that screamed, *well, I got nothing!*

"Okay," said Maya. "How soon can we leave?"

"Wait here," said Kali. "Give me an hour."

With that, Maya took a seat on the sofa with Inari resting by her feet on the floor, and Kali exited the house to make the necessary preparations. While Kali was away, Maya took the time to think a bit more about Marcus' story. She thought about all the struggles he went through and how much they correlated with her own. She wondered how things might have been different if she had allowed herself to fall into that same pit of blind madness. How tempting it might have been to just ignore the real world around you and live in a comfortable fantasy—a dangerous temptation if ever there was one, likely shared by some of the other cultists, at least at first.

Less than an hour later, Kali had made all the necessary preparations for their journey to Maya's home. The side car that attached to Kali's bike was indeed just big enough for Maya and Inari. Delroy, the soldier Maya previously had a slight altercation with just before the liberation of The Trade Post, was charged with driving Maya's Beast along with them for the journey.

Kali was conversing with Marcus, no doubt make some final preparations.

"I'll be gone two days at the most," said Kali. "You know what to do if otherwise, right?"

"Don't worry," replied Marcus, "we got this. You go do your delivery thing."

Kali laughed a little before giving Marcus a big embrace.

"See you soon," said Kali.

With everything ready to go, Kali mounted her bike with Maya and Inari already on board and checked in with Delroy, who gave a hearty thumbs up. They both cranked up some energy and headed down the road together. Maya felt a little bit weird being a passenger this time around, but she quickly got the feel of it.

"So this is what it feels like, huh," said Maya to her fox friend who was distracted, holding her face to the breeze.

The four of them were on their way to Douglass Ranch and all seemed well. Except, unbeknownst to any of them, their journey was being observed by a distant onlooker through a mighty telescope.

The Reaper, accompanied by two other cultists, was about to follow their trail.

# 14
# You Seem Familiar

It took Maya and the others a good three hours to reach Douglass Ranch: travel time plus the occasional stop to answer natures call or to wind up some kinetic energy. Maya's bruise on the left side of her face was much less noticeable and her headache had largely subsided, but she still felt occasional bouts of dizziness. *Maybe one more good night's rest will do the trick*, Maya thought to herself. In any case, she was excited to finally be returning home, even if only for a little while. After all, the Reaper (the Andy version) was still out there, and she knew that she had to take him down. But for now, she'd have to put those concerns on hold. There was stuff to be done at home first.

Soon, they reached the front fence gate entrance of Douglass Ranch. They rode their vehicles through the gate and parked them just outside the main house. As usual, the village dogs rushed over to greet

Maya a Inari, completely ignoring Kali and Delroy.

Hearing the commotion, Michael stepped outside to investigate, and was relieved to see Maya and Inari had returned. He rushed over to greet them and gave Maya the biggest bear hug possible.

"You're alive," proclaimed Michael.

"I'm so sorry I scared you," said Maya.

Dougie was not too far behind Michael and approached Maya.

"There you are, my dear," said Dougie. "Thank goodness you're back. We were all getting a bit anxious."

Maya made her apologies and briefly described the events leading up to and including the liberation of The Trade Post. Suddenly, she remembered something important.

"Oh, forgive me," said Maya as she gestured Kali to come over. "Dougie, this is…"

A sudden realization struck Maya's mind like a freight train! In the midst of all this insanity, Maya had completely forgotten that she never told Dougie anything about Kali. Yes, she had mentioned The Trade Post and that she had made a few friend there, but she had never told Dougie about Kali at all. She never thought she would ever have to. If she had remembered this really vital detail, Maya might not have agreed to letting Kali drive her home. Now that she had finally come back after unintentionally scaring Dougie, Michael, and the rest of the village, the last thing she wanted to do was place this massive burden on Dougie. At least, not right now.

Quickly, Maya improvised a solution.

"…this is Lylla," continued Maya, "my friend from The Trade Post."

Kali was understandably utterly confused, as was Delroy; she then glanced at Maya with a look that read "what's going on here?"

"Oh, *Lylla* has been so eager to meet you, *Dougie*," continued Maya, trying her best to signal Kali, "weren't you *Lylla?*"

Kali glared at Maya, to which Maya responded with her own eyes for a solid several seconds. Until, finally…

"Yes, I'm Lylla. It's great to finally meet you," said Kali, offering her hand to Dougie.

Dougie accepted and shook Kali's hand. "Glad to meet a friend of Maya".

Delroy, meanwhile, was still a bit confused.

"Hey," said Delroy to Kali, "what's going…"

Kali gave Delroy a freezing stare.

"…uh… What's going on with the smoke over there?" asked Delroy, pointing down the path.

"Oh, that's Joseph's station," replied Maya. "He's our local blacksmith."

"Ah," responded Delroy, "I hear you!"

"I'm glad you took the time to help my dear Maya," said Dougie.

"Oh, it was a mutual pleasure," replied Kali.

Dougie looked deeper into Kali's eyes.

"You seem… familiar," said Dougie. "Have we perhaps met before?"

Kali scrambled in her mind to come up with an evasive answer.

"Uh… maybe in another lifetime," joked Kali. *That's more true than not.*

An awkward pause fell on the scene. Maya was just about to try and break the silence with a fake laugh when…

"Inari!!!"

The voice turned out to be little Izzy, who was suddenly charging toward them, making a beeline for the fox. Inari, upon hearing Izzy's voice, ran to her, leaped into her arms, and slathered the little girl with affectionate licks to the face. Izzy responded in kind with pats and loving words.

In the ensuing silence: "Well," said Michael, "you must all be hungry. Please, come inside. I've got supper in the works."

"Oh, no," said Kali, "thank you, but we wouldn't want to impose."

"Please, my dear," said Dougie, "it's the least we can do. Besides, I'm sure you have some interesting stories to tell about your time with Maya, don't you?"

"Oh, no," said Maya in as calm a tone as she could muster, "they really should be going."

"I insist," retorted Dougie.

With that, Michael and Dougie headed toward the house. When they were out of earshot, Kali placed her hand on Maya's shoulder with a firm grip.

"You owe me," said Kali, "big time!"

Kali then walked toward the house, making delightful banter about how grateful she was to be invited for dinner. Meanwhile, Maya stood there somewhat annoyed with herself—a sentiment shared by Delroy.

"Okay," said Delroy, "you gonna tell me just what the hell that was?"

Maya let out a small sigh.

"There are still some things I haven't told Dougie about just yet," said Maya, "and I would like it to stay that way for now, if you please."

"Wow," quipped Delroy, "I knew you had guts, but this is something else!"

Delroy then patted Maya on the back and went toward the house.

Maya stood there sulking for a moment before Inari, having enjoyed a quick bit of play with little Izzy, came up to Maya with a concerned look in her dual-colored eyes.

"It's okay, girl," said Maya, "for now, anyway."

After a few more moments, Maya and Inari finally made their way inside.

# 15
# Chance Encounters

Later that night, sometime after a somewhat awkward dinner, sprinkled with conversational gaps, an impromptu meeting was held in Dougie's house at Maya's insistence. The gathering basically entailed Maya apologizing to the various village council leaders for her sudden and unexpected absence.

In the immediate aftermath of the Wave, when it became clear that non-biological electricity could no longer be generated or replicated anywhere on the planet, most governments had no contingency plan in place for such an event. Any plans they did have were drafted with the assumption that power would eventually be restored. Therefore, people were suddenly compelled to build their own forms of organization, cut adrift from the centuries of familiar governmental rules and regulations. Most villages, like Douglass Ranch, adopted a council-style form of government: representatives of essential tasks required for functional survival (farming, medicine, hunting and gathering, etc.) regularly met to discuss issues that needed to be addressed and to provide progress reports on their respective topics of expertise.

At the meeting, Maya proceeded to explain the events that had transpired at The Trade Post and the battle against the Dreaded Dragon cult. While she was able to assure them that the cultists were not likely coming their way anytime soon, she did emphasize the need for extra security and asked the council leaders to ready themselves and the rest of the village to either defend or evacuate.

After the meeting slowly dissolved, the council leaders went about their tasks of preparing the village and their constituents. Under Maya's prior two years of leadership, everyone in the village had learned some variation of self-defense and had been drilled on specific emergencies, such as raider attacks, and evacuation procedures. Now, all that was needed to put the village on high alert was about an hours preparation. By sunset, all of Douglass Ranch was prepared for whatever or whoever might try to disturb their peaceful home.

As everything toned down for the night, Maya offered Kali (a.k.a. Lylla) and Delroy one of the presently unused cabins in the village as a place to sleep for the night. The previous occupants had moved out not too long ago and had willed it to the village for general use. It was lightly furnished with two beds, a coffee table, and some stools. Once everyone was settled in, they all prepared for a good night's sleep. Maya was not only grateful to be back in her own bed once again but was hopeful that this would be the last night's sleep she would need for her headaches and bouts of dizziness to finally subside.

As the night drew on, and the whole village found itself in peaceful slumber, Kali found herself restless! Even as she learned the patterns of the night patrol's torch lights winding all around the village, and felt secure enough inside the cabin, she still couldn't find herself able to fall asleep, unlike Delroy who was already sleeping like a log!

After a few hours of futile dozing, Kali decided to step outside for some air. She carefully got out of bed, tiptoed to the door, put on her heavy coat, and stepped outside, closing the door gently behind her.

As Kali stood there watching the torches of the night watchers float by, she noticed how they almost resembled fireflies. Then, as her thoughts continued to run away with her, she was suddenly struck with memories of the arrow that struck down the guard on the morning of the invasion. That single image of a man she cared for being suddenly taken down by the Dreaded Dragons like a hunting prize haunted her thoughts still. It was a heavy image that made her shake her head in frustration, trying to move her thoughts onto something else.

Just then…

"I see you can't sleep either, Lylla," said a voice from the shadows.

"Who's there?" asked Kali, reflexively reaching for her six-shooter only to realize she hadn't brought it with her outside.

"Oh, just an old lady out for a little night stroll," said the voice.

The source of the voice moved out of the shadows and revealed itself to be Dougie, who was also wearing a heavy coat and wandering about with her walking stick. Kali was relieved but not fully at ease.

"Oh, good evening," said Kali. "You spooked me a little just now."

"I've been known to have that effect on people sometimes," joked Dougie.

The two women stood in each other's company for a moment, uncertain of what to say.

"You know," said Dougie, "you remind me of someone I once knew a long time ago."

" I do?" asked Kali.

"Yes," said Dougie. "She was just a little girl when last I saw her. She'd probably be about your age now. I don't know if she's still with us, you see."

Kali didn't think there was any kind of subtext to Dougie's words, but she still played along as Dougie conversed.

"She was the granddaughter," continued Dougie, "of… someone I once cared a great deal about."

"Once?" inquired Kali.

Dougie looked at Kali with a kind of gentle stare that implied something more important was lurking under the surface.

"Yes," Dougie finally said. "He made a choice that… I didn't agree with at the time. But I've come to appreciate the life it has given me. I wonder if that little girl would feel the same?"

Kali hesitated at first, instinctively wanting to retreat into the cabin. However, despite the unusual circumstances of their… chance encounter, Kali felt in her heart that she needed to respond in some way.

"Well," said Kali, "I suppose that if she were here, she might admit how angry and afraid she was, and how she felt robbed of her own future—that is, until, she met someone who showed her something better and… gave her the choice that she never had. And I suppose she would be grateful to that person, and would call her a friend."

Dougie closed her eyes and nodded her head, as if a massive weight had been lifted off her shoulders.

"If that were the case," said Dougie, "I think I would tell her… how sorry I am… and how hopeful I am for her future."

Kali smiled at the kind old woman as they shared an unexpected, pleasant moment together.

"I think she'd be grateful to hear that."

A peaceful silence sealed their respective, quiet realizations.

"Well, said Dougie, "I should get back inside and try to get some sleep."

"Please," said Kali, "let me walk with you."

"You're too kind, my dear," replied Dougie.

The two women enjoyed a brief stroll down the pathway and back to Dougie's house.

"Get some good rest," said Kali as she helped Dougie up the small flight of stairs to the door.

"Oh, I think I will tonight, my dear," said Dougie with a smile.

Kali smiled back.

"Well, good night."

Kali turned to make her way back down the path toward her guest cabin.

"Your grandfather would be proud of you," said Dougie.

Kali stopped in her tracks and looked back at Dougie. At first, she was annoyed at the notion that Dougie knew exactly who she really was but chose to go along with Maya's dumb façade for whatever reason. But, as Kali looked at

Dougie's genuine and warm smile, even in the cold night air, her heart warmed with a feeling of deep appreciation and relief.

Taking it all in, Kali smiled back at Dougie as she placed her hand over her heart. In that moment, it seemed that two weights had been lifted from Kali's shoulders as well.

Kali lingered on the path for a bit longer as she watched Dougie enter the house, wanting to ensure she was indeed now out of the cold. Kali returned to her cabin and soon felt more relaxed, allowing herself to fall into a deep and satisfying sleep.

The next morning, Maya and Michael treated everyone to a full and delightful breakfast: complete with fresh coffee, fruit, and pastries. The whole gang enjoyed a pleasant morning of good food, thoughtful conversation, and laughs. After everyone's bellies were full, Kali and Delroy packed their belongings and prepared for the ride back to The Trade Post. Delroy felt a bit weird having to ride passenger. His uncomfortable remarks were met with a simple nod from Maya, as if to say, "I know."

Maya gave Kali a great hug for the road.

"Thank you for everything, " said Maya. "You be safe out there, you hear?"

"Don't worry," replied Kali. "We'll be fine."

Kali started cranking up some energy for her bike.

"Just remember," said Kali with a smile, "you still owe me big."

Shortly, Kali built up enough energy, and the two of them hit the road for their return home. Maya and the others waved them both a hearty farewell and kept watching them speed down the road until they were out of sight. With that, they all went about their various tasks for the day.

About an hour into the drive, Kali noticed something strange up the road. A pack of old cars blocked their path. This wasn't too alarming at first since older cars on the roads tended to get moved around sometimes by nature or by other travelers, but Kali distinctly remembered this particular stretch of the road being totally clear when they last rode down here.

"Look alive," said Kali to her companion Delroy. "Something's not right!"

Delroy brought himself to full alert, concentrating on the cars ahead.

Preferring to not stop her bike, Kali looked ahead and around the area and determined that there did not appear to be any apparent danger.

Coming to a complete stop at the little pile of old cars blocking the way, Kali kept the kinetic motor running as she further evaluated the situation before her. The cars in front of them appeared to be light enough for her and Delroy to push by hand. That's when she suddenly noticed something.

All along the ground close to the strangely positioned old cars were footprints. Upon observation, their pattern and freshness suggested these cars had been deliberately moved to block the road. This was an ambush!

In a flash, Kali turned around her bike and speeded away in the opposite direction as quickly as possible. She only traveled maybe fifty yards from the road block when…

SWOOSH!

A long pole shot out from close to the ground and embedded itself straight through the front wheel of Kali's bike, causing the entire vehicle to flip into the air. The centrifugal force was enough to throw Kali out of her seat, flinging her in the opposite direction of the bike's trajectory. Much to her horror, she was suddenly suspended in space. Even worse, for a brief moment, she could see Delroy still inside the passenger car, seemingly trapped.

With a massive thud, Kali hit the ground rolling out of control. She tried her best to protect herself by holding her arms out close to her face, but that movement only seemed to make things worse. The force of the fall coupled with the momentum from being thrown off the seat made every subsequent tumble hurt more than the last. Kali was fortunate enough for her momentum to stop moments before her bike finally hit the ground and rolled further down the road.

Kali laid on the ground, too shocked to move. She couldn't even muster the energy to lift her head to see how bad the damage was or if Delroy was somehow still alive. All she could do was lie there and listen to the hunk of metal rattle and roll its way down the road until gravity finally caught up to it, forcing the once elegant ride to now crumble into a pile of scrap.

Kali tried to call out to Delroy in the thin hope that he somehow had survived, but the wind was knocked clear out of her. The best she could muster was a faint and raspy croak.

"Delroy," gasped Kali, doing her damnedest to gather more air into her lungs.

Seconds later, Kali could hear footsteps approaching her. They were slow and deliberate. At first, Kali hoped it was indeed Delroy, fighting through his injuries and making his way over to check on her.

Sadly, she was instead met with a haunting and dismal sight.

It was the Reaper, standing directly over Kali's wounded body. Kali could only stare back in horror as she continued to gasp for breath. Fighting through the pain in her body, Kali managed to draw her six-shooter and tried to take aim, but the Reaper slammed his foot down onto Kali's hand, crushing her fingers against the handle of the gun. Kali struggled to scream as her lungs desperately tried to take in breath.

A moment later, the Reaper lifted his foot, allowing one of his goons to retrieve the six-shooter, while a second goon loaded his arm-mounted crossbow and aimed it directly at Kali's head.

The Reaper leaned in and grabbed Kali's face, forcing her gaze to meet his.

"Breathe," commanded the Reaper through his helmet. "Just breathe!"

Slowly, hesitantly, Kali managed to regain her breath, and started breathing normally.

"There you go," said the Reaper with a sarcastically menacing tone.

Kali continued to fight through the pain as she struggled to speak.

"Andy," grunted Kali.

The Reaper kept his helmeted gaze on Kali's terrified face. Then, very deliberately, the Reaper removed his helmet, revealing his true face to Kali.

"So you do remember me," said Andy.

The two goonish cultists, realizing their Dear Leader had inexplicably removed his helmet, looked away in absolute terror, falling to the ground and covering their faces with their hands.

"Oh, please, Dear Leader," said one of the cultists, "spare me! I didn't see anything!"

The other cultist was also writhing on the ground, proclaiming the same absence of guilt.

The Reaper then stood up, still without his helmet, and drew his sword. He first went over to the cultist who had retrieved Kali's six-shooter. The Reaper picked up the gun, examined it, and placed it into his belt.

"You served your purpose well, my child," said the Reaper.

Suddenly, the Reaper plunged his blade into the cultist's back with deadly force.

Kali watched, no longer in terror. Her past had literally caught up to her, and it was angry!

The other cultist (who moments ago had been aiming his arm-mounted crossbow at Kali) despite not looking at anything for fear of seeing what he ought not to see, could clearly hear what sounded like Dear Leader's sword tearing through flesh. The sound alone was enough to petrify him entirely.

The Reaper approached the other cultist. With tremendous force he grabbed the cultist's arm, forcing it away from his face. The cultist squeezed his eyes shut, tighter than he ever had before.

"Open your eyes," commanded the Reaper.

"I can't," said the cultist.

"You defy my orders?" asked The Reaper.

"No, never," replied the cultist.

"Then open your eyes!"

Slowly, hesitantly, the cultist did as he had been commanded and opened his eyes. His heart nearly stopped as he found himself looking directly into Dear Leader's penetrating stare and ghoulish grin.

"You've seen my face," said the Reaper. "I do not deem you worthy. You know what you must do?"

The cultist was too petrified to speak.

"Answer me," demanded the Reaper.

"…Yes," finally said the cultist.

The Reaper let go of the cultist's arm.

"Then, do it," ordered the Reaper.

The cultist, despite his fearful state, and much to Kali's surprise, took his arm-mounted-crossbow, aimed it directly under his chin, and fired the bolt straight through his head, killing himself. His body fell to the ground close to Kali, who by now was more shocked than in pain from her massive tumble.

The Reaper hovered over Kali's anguished face.

"You see," said the Reaper, "you thought you killed a man. But instead, you created a god!"

With spectacular strength and appalling apathy, the Reaper ripped Kali from the ground, flung her over his shoulder, and carried her away. Kali was too weak and in too much pain to resist, despite how much she so desperately wanted to.

After the Reaper had ridden off with Kali, a figure emerged from underneath the remaining rubble of Kali's bike like a zombie rising from the grave. It was Delroy, somehow still alive but with many broken parts—most notably his very dislocated left shoulder. Biting through the pain, Delroy forced the bone back into place and used his belt as a makeshift sling for his arm. Despite all of this, Delroy fought through it all as he shuffled his way back toward Douglass Ranch.

# 16
# Change of Plans

Later that same afternoon back at Douglass Ranch, Michael and Izzy were packing up their vehicle for their own journey back home to Ashland. Maya, Inari, Dougie, and Charlie were there to see them off. Maya was so grateful to them both for staying so much longer than planned and for helping out in so many ways. She was sorry to see them go—although perhaps not as much as Inari was sorry to see little Izzy have to leave. And here Maya thought she was the only one for Inari.

"I can't thank you enough for all your kind assistance here," said Maya as she embraced Michael.

"It's alright," replied Michael. "Sometimes, where you are is where you're needed most."

As Michael finished packing up the bike, he began to crank up some energy.

"Izzy," called out Michael, "it's time to go!"

Izzy was giving Inari one last loving pat on the head after they just played a quick round of chase.

"I have to go home now, girl," said Izzy to the fox. "I'll see you again sometime soon. I love you!"

Izzy ran to her father and jumped into the side car.

"Seatbelt," said Michael.

Izzy strapped herself into the seat.

The two of them said their final goodbyes before driving down the same dirt path where they had seen Kali and Delroy off just a few hours earlier.

Maya, Dougie, and Charlie all waved at Michael and Izzy until they could no longer see them down the road. With that, the trio went back to their daily tasks.

Sometime later, Maya was up in her room at her work desk. Littered all throughout the surface were documents she had taken from The Trade Post: scout reports and spy intel regarding the Dreaded Dragons from the past, a couple of recently printed books about some of the cults in the new world, a few maps, and some crude sketches of possible defense plans for her home village.

As Maya looked over the voluminous information she had laid out before her, she began to wonder if the entire region of Crescent City had been effectively taken in by the cult or if it was just a smallish group that had taken over a small town through fear and force. If it was the former, then it might be a greater challenge to combat them should they try another strike on The Trade Post, or any other village for that matter. If, however, it was the latter, then perhaps there was a reason for a different approach entirely.

Maya combed through every bit of intel she had at her disposal, searching for something that could help her make a better-informed decision. Although much of the information was helpful, none of it had yet provided her with what she really needed to know. It seemed that the only way she might find out what she really needed would be to travel to Crescent City herself and learn firsthand just what she was dealing with, a prospect that both scared her and piqued her curiosity. After all, most of what she understood about the Dreaded Dragons and their isolated hometown was based on speculation and hazy memories from travelers who hadn't ventured far into the cult's town. Maya mused on the fact that even Marcus found recollections of his time there somewhat foggy and for understandable reasons. Still, if she needed a guide, there was no one better.

While contemplating all of these possibilities, Maya decided to take a sip from her little coffee cup, only to find it empty. Deciding that it was about time for a short break, Maya took her cup downstairs to the kitchen. Upon reaching the bottom of the stairs, she heard what sounded like typing coming from Dougie's study. Curious and not wanting to disturb whatever might be going on, Maya quietly made her way to the study's entrance.

As she peeked in around the corner, she saw Dougie sitting at her desk typing away on her old typewriter—no doubt the same one she had used for the clue letters she had typed for Maya's previous journey north. Maya wondered what Dougie was writing, or to whom she was writing, but she knew better than to pry. So Maya left Dougie to her own devices and went back into the kitchen.

As Maya went about the task of preparing her coffee ritual, she was suddenly distracted by what was most certainly an approaching vehicle coming from outside the main entrance to the village. Concerned and bit confused, Maya set down her coffee-making tools and rushed outside toward the entrance. Inari, who'd been wondering around the village for a moment, saw Maya walking toward the road. Sensing that something might be amiss, she ran straight to her best friend and was by her side in a matter of seconds.

Once the two of them were at the main entrance, Maya looked down the road to try and see what it might be. Her initial fear was that the Reaper had found her home and was already on his way back for revenge, but that couldn't be. Even if he knew where her home was, there's no way he could have already massed another small army for his personal crusade. Nevertheless, that remote possibility overwhelmed Maya's mind and heart, and she was preparing herself for if she had to start alerting the village to the impending danger!

Just a second later, Maya saw a glimpse of what was approaching the village. It became close enough for Maya to make out what it was.

It was Michael, riding down the road on his kinetic bike with little Izzy in his lap. *Why isn't she in the side car?* Maya thought to herself. *Wait, what the...* Maya could see someone else in the side car. *Is that... Delroy?*

Maya and Inari ran up the road toward the approaching vehicle. They got maybe ten yards past the entrance gate before meeting up with Michael and the others.

"Michael," cried Maya, "what happened?"

Without waiting for a reply, Maya checked on Delroy in the side car. Michael dismounted his vehicle with Izzy in his arms. When he saw Inari standing by, Michael gently placed Izzy down next to the fox. Izzy wrapped her arms around the fox, afraid and confused about what was going on. Inari sat in place, making comforting noises to try and calm the little girl the best she could. Inari then gave a quick glance to Michael as if to say, "I got this." Michael, feeling assured about Izzy's well being, went over to help Maya with Delroy.

Michael started to lift Delroy out of the side car to carry him into the village.

"No," shouted Maya, "don't move him anymore just yet! Go get some water and the doctor!"

"Right," responded Michael as he ran down the road to do as he had been told.

Maya looked over Delroy. He was pretty beaten up and broken down, his head bobbing back and forth trying to stay conscious.

"That's it, Delroy," said Maya, "stay with me. Don't conk out on me now!"

"Kali…" whispered Delroy in a weak voice.

"What?" asked Maya.

"The… Reaper… has… Kali."

Maya's heart just about stopped. The news made her stand up and look down the road where Kali had just left a few hours ago. The fear of what might be coming next activated Maya to her very core!

# 17
# A Cold War

Delroy was recovering in the village's infirmary, overseen by Dr. Ramona. Maya had grown a fast friendship with the good doctor ever since Dougie's near-fatal heart attack two years ago. Although Dougie had still technically been in charge of Douglass Ranch while Maya was away on her mission to seek out the Machine (the device behind the Wave, eliminating the worlds non-biological electricity), it was Dr. Ramona who acted as the unofficial leader, willingly relieving Dougie of some of her more burdensome responsibilities as her health gradually recovered. Dr. Ramona's authority in the village as chief medical counselor further cemented her abilities as a doctor and as a standing leader in times of crisis.

According to Dr. Ramona's examination, Delroy was extremely lucky. Despite suffering a dislocated shoulder, three broken ribs, several lacerations and bruises, and a mild concussion, Delroy didn't appear to have any signs of internal bleeding or organ damage—at least, not within the ability of the good Doctor's skills and available equipment. While he was being treated, Delroy explained what happened to him and Kali as best he could to Maya: how it all happened so quickly and how Kali seemed to recognize The Reaper in an unexpected way. He even managed to recount the freaky behavior of the other cultists upon seeing the Reaper's uncovered face!

Once Delroy was tended to and resting, Maya went back to her house to check in with everyone else. Michael was on the sofa, holding onto little Izzy, who was still traumatized by the event. Inari stayed close, also doing her part to help comfort the little girl. Meanwhile, Dougie took it upon herself to bake something nice for Izzy, with the help of Maya's little brother, Charlie.

Maya went back to her room's work bench where she had just been reviewing all the information at her disposal. Now with the knowledge of Kali's kidnapping, the Reaper's true identity, the cultists' insanely fanatical devotion to their Dear Leader, and all of the possibilities presented by this myriad of facts, there was one absolutely undeniable thing that had to happen: Kali had to be rescued, and the Reaper needed to be taken down permanently!

If he managed to find the Machine and somehow gain access to its systems, he would become nearly absolutely powerful in so many ways. It would be a reign of terror unlike anything else in human history. The Reaper could control not only the people but technology, both old and potentially new. He could hold the fate of all humanity in his hands. *This must not happen,* screamed Maya to herself.

With this sudden resolution, Maya took out one of the old maps of Northern California and Southern Oregon. She found Crescent City and marked it with a big red circle. She searched the map for a specific spot that could serve as a potential rendezvous ground. Her first step was to send word to Marcus back at The Trade Post via her own messenger raven, instructing Marcus to ready his troops for a special assault on the cult's compound to rescue Kali and neutralize the Reaper!

According to a map drawn by Marcus previously seen by Maya, the Dreaded Dragons' stronghold was located in a small, dilapidated suburban neighborhood next to the local lake, known as Lake Earl. The actual urban area of Crescent City was mostly abandoned, like so many other cities and densely populated areas after the Wave made then-modern lifestyles inhospitable.

Once Maya had finalized her plans, she wrote the message with instructions, rolled it up, picked up her messenger raven, whispered the destination to the bird, then launched the black flyer into the sky. She watched as it glided in the air in the direction of The Trade Post.

After that, Maya went door to door through the village, informing everyone of another emergency meeting for later that night, instructing those in charge of the tent area to set it up for later on. As the village prepared for the upcoming emergency meeting (again), Maya went straight back to her house. She was pleased to find Michael, Izzy, Dougie, and Charlie enjoying one of Dougie's famous pumpkin pies. Even Inari was enjoying a decent serving of the tasty treat.

Maya drew close to Izzy with a gentle demeanor.

"Hey, sweetheart," said Maya, "how are you feeling?"

"Okay," said Izzy.

"You've had one heck of a bad day, huh?"

"Yeah, but it's okay."

Maya was amazed at little Izzy's resilience.

"You've got a brave one here," said Maya to Michael as he scarfed down a bite of pie.

"Don't I know it," responded Michael.

Comforted and calmed by Izzy's improved state, Maya cut herself a slice of pie and joined the others at the table.

"Okay," said Maya, "I need you all to listen to me, please."

Everyone at the table, including Inari, gave Maya their complete attention.

"There's going to be another emergency meeting tonight at the Center Tent. I'll be announcing my plans to tackle this… issue with the Dreaded Dragons."

"What can I do to help?" asked Michael.

"Nothing. You've already done too much for me, for us. All you need to do is get yourself and Izzy safely back home."

Maya went on to explain part of her plan for Michael and Izzy's safe return home: At dawn tomorrow, Maya, Inari, Michael and Izzy would head north for The Trade Post. Once there, they would meet up with a few soldiers, who would escort Michael and Izzy back to their home in Ashland.

"But what about you?" asked Michael.

"I'll be heading west to meet up with some friends who will help me complete the mission."

Michael deeply opposed the idea of letting Maya run into the fire essentially on her own, even though she made it pretty clear that she wouldn't be.

"Okay," said Michael, "then who's going to be in charge while you're away?"

Dougie then put her plate down onto the coffee table.

"I think that duty should fall onto me," said Dougie. "I've been in charge before, I'm confident I can handle it for a little while again."

"Actually," said Maya, "I was thinking about putting Dr. Ramona in temporary charge during my absence."

A surprised look flashed immediately onto Dougie's face.

"She's experienced," continued Maya, "organized, and she's prepared. She and I had a conversation about this some time ago, as part of a contingency plan I put in place for situations like this."

"Well, my dear," said Dougie, "you have been quite busy!"

"Yes," replied Maya, "I have been busy, and we need to have a proper conversation about this before I make my final decision."

Dougie let out a sigh of contented relief.

"Very well, my dear."

"Okay, fine," said Michael, relieved that the difficulty between Maya and Dougie had been resolved. "I can go along with not being around, but what exactly is the big picture here? What is it you're not telling us?"

Maya took a moment to consider what to say next. Under the present circumstances, she knew that Dougie and Michael deserved to know the full truth of what was happening and what she needed to do to fix it. But it meant revealing something massively complex to them both. Maybe it wasn't as massive as what they already knew, but it was of major significance all the same. In this dark moment, Maya knew she needed to tell them what they needed to hear: the truth.

"Charlie," said Maya calling upon her little brother, "would you please take Izzy to the gardens for a bit? I need the two of you to pick some strawberries for me."

"But why?" asked Charlie.

"Because I'm going to make some strawberry pancakes tomorrow!"

"Really?" asked Charlie with an anticipatory twinkle in his eye.

"Really," confirmed Maya.

Charlie did as he was told and asked Michael's permission to take Izzy with him to the gardens. Michael looked over at Maya who returned his gaze with a stern look that read, "please trust me," before permitting Izzy to go with Charlie. Once the children were out of the house, leaving Maya alone with Michael and Dougie, she took a deep breath and said what she had to say.

"The woman I introduced as 'Lylla' yesterday, that's not her name. Her real name is Kali… Kali Clarke! She knows about the Machine"

Michael's face was slapped with a look of shock, while Dougie merely looked on unfazed.

Maya went on to explain the events of that day two years ago—how she confronted Kali at the location of the Machine, how they came to realize the choice they had to make together, and how they came to their agreement about where to go from there. She then went on to tell them that the Reaper just kidnapped her and very likely planned to interrogate her for the location of The Machine. Maya further explained her plan to rescue Kali, take down the Reaper and, if she was lucky, disband the entire Dreaded Dragon cult!

Silence.

"I'm sorry I never told you about her, Dougie," said Maya. "I didn't want you to worry about it anymore. That's my job now!"

"I knew it," proclaimed Dougie.

"Knew what?"

"That she was Dr. Clarke's granddaughter. I never told her I knew; I merely… implied."

Maya was just as surprised as Michael was about this revelation.

"But why?"

"Because, my dear, I was relieved to know that she found a better life and that you gave her what she had been denied: a choice."

Michael suddenly chimed in.

"I'm sorry, but getting back to the subject at hand, assuming the Reaper learns the location of the Machine, can he even use it?"

"No," replied Maya. "The Machine is harmless without the proper instructions on how to access it, which I alone have the ciphered instructions for, and the key to unlock the cypher is located at the Machine. But without the cypher, the key is useless!"

A sigh of relief emanated from both Dougie and Michael.

"The good news is," continued Maya, "the Reaper doesn't know that, at least not yet. Which is why I will need to rescue Kali before the Reaper has the chance to break her!"

Michael hesitated for a bit before formulating his next question.

"I, uh, I hate to be the morbid one here, but, what if the Reaper's already broken Kali?"

"Trust me," replied Maya, "Kali is much stronger than you might think!"

A moment of silence cloaked the room as Dougie and Michael tried to absorb everything that had just been shared with them.

"Look," said Maya, "I know this is a lot to take in, and I am deeply sorry to place this burden on you both, but you deserved to know the truth, now more than ever, and I need you both to please believe that I only want to do what's right!"

Dougie and Michael looked at each other for a moment, exchanging a cool and heavily loaded glance. Then, Michael got up from his seat, approached Maya, kneeled before her, and placed his hands on her shoulders.

"You don't have to carry this burden alone anymore," said Michael. "I may not appreciate how I know the truth, but I am glad to know it from you."

Maya smiled at Michael's sincerity with a few tears of deep relief and appreciation in her eyes.

"And from you," said Michael looking at Dougie.

Dougie also shed a few tears.

"If I'm going to put my faith in anyone for the future," continued Michael, returning his attention to Maya, "for *Izzy's* future, I will gladly put it in you!"

With that, Michael gave Maya the biggest and most sincere embrace that she could have possibly ever had from him. A moment later, Dougie joined in, as did Inari, and the light of their love brightened up the room!

Later that evening, during the meeting, Maya did as she planned. She informed the village of a potential threat to their peaceful lives and her plans to do something about it herself, leaving the good Dr. Ramona in charge during her absence, and promising the whole village she would return once the threat had been neutralized. The people of Douglass Ranch cheered and proclaimed their faith in Maya, and all swore to do their part!

Before turning in for the evening, Maya had her important conversation with Dougie, as promised, about who was to be in charge during her absence. While Maya trusted her great aunt's ability to resume her former duties as village leader, Maya also recognized some of Dougie's limitations imposed by the systemic damages arising from her previous heart attack. Instead, Maya wanted Dougie to focus her energy on caring for Charlie, trusting Dougie's ability to keep him occupied and calm during Maya's next bout of sudden absence. Without question, Dougie gladly accepted her familiar responsibility.

    The next morning, as promised, Maya treated everyone to a lovely strawberry pancake breakfast. Afterward, Maya and Michael prepared themselves for the journey. Maya outfitted Inari with her tactical vest and all of its gear, placing her fox friend in full mission mode. She also let Inari ride in the sidecar with Izzy for the trip to The Trade Post.

    With their gear primed and their hearts committed, Maya led the way up the road toward their first destination.

    Operation Dragons's Lair had just begun!

# 18
# Forged in Fire

The ride to The Trade Post took Maya and the others three hours or so, not counting the time spent removing the cars that had initially blocked Kali's path the day before and the time spent for the occasional break to re-crank energy for the vehicles. Once they arrived at The Trade Post, they were greeted by Marcus and some of his best soldiers, providing everyone with a warm welcome.

Marcus and Maya shared a fond embrace.

"How's Delroy?" asked Marcus. "Is he still alive?"

"He was when I left," replied Maya. "He's still recovering. Took a hell of a beating, but he's tougher than you think. He told me to tell you he hasn't forgotten you still owe him his winning from the last poker game."

Marcus exploded with a reassured guffaw at Maya's remarks.

"That sounds like Delroy!"

As Michael checked in with his assigned escorts, Maya shared a few words with him before his departure.

"You good?" asked Maya.

"Never better," replied Michael.

"Don't forget to look into that thing I asked you about," said Maya rather nonchalantly.

"You got it," replied Michael, "though, I got to be honest, I never took you for a girl who was interested in getting one of those."

"Oh, it's not for me," said Maya as she nodded her head towards Marcus. "It's for him."

Michael seemed even more confused.

"You'll understand later," said Maya, "I promise."

Michael responded to Maya's statement with a confused smile and a little giggle.

As planned, two of Marcus' soldiers were prepped and ready to escort Michael and Izzy directly back to their home in Ashland. Maya gave Michael a massive bear hug, thanking him for everything he'd done and promising to repay him in some way. Izzy gave a big goodbye hug to Inari before giving one to Maya as well. With little Izzy secured in the sidecar and Michael cranking more juice for the trip, the two of them and their escorts rode off toward Ashland.

Once they were on their way, Maya and Marcus immediately got to work on finalizing their preparations for Operation Dragon's Lair. According to Marcus' recollection, along with some additional intel they had managed to get out of their cultist prisoner still in their custody, the Dreaded Dragon's compound consisted of a few blocks of old houses in the old suburbs. All of them were overseen by the Reaper from his fortified mansion located at the farthest end of the old suburb, closest to the lake. No one except the Reaper and his immediate servants, not even Marcus, has ever been inside the mansion, so they would have to move in quickly as well as carefully when they arrived.

The plan was simple: sneak into the compound under the cover of night, break into the mansion, find Kali, get her out, bring down the Reaper, and come home. If they left within the hour they would likely reach their designated spot to set up their base of operations in four hours. After one last check of all their gear and weapons, everyone mounted their vehicles and hit the road.

The path to Crescent City wasn't too arduous but it wasn't a breeze through the woods either. For the most part they were able to travel on the old roads with little in the way of obstacles—that is, until they came across some remains of a few fallen trees or boulders that caused them to go off-road from time to time. Thankfully, everyone in the party had enough experience handling themselves in these kinds of situations—Maya especially, who spent considerable amounts of her free time back home practicing her driving techniques, perfecting her off-road abilities.

After about two hours of riding, Marcus called for a water break. They found a good spot off the side of to the old road to stop.

"Five minutes," said Marcus to the gang as they took a few welcome sips from their canteens.

Maya managed to pull out a metal bowl from her stuffed saddle bag, poured some water into it, and offered it to Inari. As the Fox enjoyed her drink, Maya took a few swigs herself from her canteen. As she rehydrated, she noticed Marcus walking farther up the road and looking down the path, almost as if he was looking for something or someone specific. Out of curiosity Maya took it upon herself to walk over to him and see what was up.

When Maya got close enough, she could almost feel the tension emanating from Marcus.

"Want a sip?" asked Maya, offering her canteen.

"No, I'm good," replied Marcus.

There was a brief moment of silence between the two of them.

"Something on your mind?" asked Maya.

Marcus didn't reply.

"Don't worry," continued Maya. "I won't tell anyone. I'm good at keeping secrets."

Marcus' eyes remained locked down the road ahead of them.

"I haven't been back there since that night," said Marcus, "since I lost her."

Maya looked at Marcus with compassionate eyes.

"I suppose I should be glad," continued Marcus, "that the 'original' Reaper is, in all likelihood, already dead. But I've wanted nothing more in this world than to look that bastard in the eyes. as I ended him myself! Made him feel the pain he caused me!"

Maya could feel Marcus' hurtful anguish. She knew all too well the pain of loss and how much it can define and defeat you, if you let it.

"When my mom died," said Maya, "I was only a teenager. I was suddenly responsible for taking care of my baby brother. Sure, my great aunt was there, and she did her damnedest for us, but I had to grow up a lot sooner than I was prepared for."

Suddenly, Marcus' eyes left the path before them and found themselves drawn to Maya and her words.

"I was so angry that she was gone," continued Maya, "and I felt like a horrible person for being angry in the first place."

Marcus knew exactly what Maya was talking about.

"But eventually," continued Maya, "I realized that… even when the ones we care about are no longer with us, their love never leaves. It stays here, with us, and, sometimes…"

Maya looked back at Inari, who was, rather unsurprisingly, making friends with the other soldiers through play. Bringing a smile to Maya's face.

"...it comes back to you in unexpected ways!"

Marcus also looked over at Inari playing with the soldiers with a sense admiration, before bringing his attention back to Maya. For a moment, Marcus felt exactly what Maya had just described—a fleeting realization that brought him a little clarity.

Marcus suddenly remembered the time limit he had imposed on the gang.

"Alright, guys, let's get back to it," ordered Marcus as he returned to his vehicle.

Maya took one last quick glance up the road before returning to her ATV.

"Hang on, Kali! We're coming for you!"

# 19
# The Belly of the Beast

Kali slowly became conscious of herself, dragging herself awake, sensing her totally sore body, and suffering a massive headache, topped off like a rotten cherry with the smell of blood and sweat assaulting her nostrils. As unfortunate as all that was, it wasn't nearly as unsettling as her surroundings. Kali found herself in a gloomy and musty room, like some kind of basement or old garage, illuminated feebly by a handful of candles scattered in a few spots throughout the claustrophobic space—which, with her vision still blurred, looked like flares of light in a night sky.

As the fuzziness cleared up, Kali could make out things in greater detail. The space was perhaps two-hundred-square feet. The walls appeared to be dark grey cement, cracked and flaking in spots from years of disrepair. Aside from the candles, the only other source of light was the sliver of sunlight beaming down from atop a flight of stairs on the opposite side of the room. Very little in the way of furniture: a few random chairs, a rusty metal table, and the rickety old cot Kali found herself lying on. On closer inspection, Kali saw that her left ankle was chained to an anchor embedded deeply in the floor. If she had any strength to speak of, she might have tried tugging at it.

Instead, she settled for struggling to sit upright. As she did so, she noticed her wounds had been treated, barely. While she thankfully didn't appear to have any broken bones, she did have a couple of lacerations that continued to ooze a bit through her bandages. *That explains the blood smell,* Kali thought to herself.

Kali tried to shout for someone who might be nearby, only to be hit with a painfully parched throat. As she looked around a bit more, she noticed a small bottle of water on the floor next to the cot. With all her strength, she bit through the pain, grabbed the bottle, yanked off the lid, and poured the wondrous liquid down her gullet like a waterfall. It hurt more to swallow than it did to speak, but she didn't care. This was a unique reprieve from the mysterious hell she found herself in!

After downing the entire bottle, there was a loud thud from across the room. Kali's attention was immediately focused. Soon after came the sound of rattling metal and chains, followed by the sound of a creaking door. The sound was so ominous that it made Kali's neck hairs stand on end, not at all helped by the sound of heavy footsteps descending the stairs.

First there was a visible foot followed by the other, then the legs, the body, and finally the head. It was the Reaper, clad in his full armor regalia, helmet and all! The Reaper slowly approached Kali like a panther stalking its prey, picking up one of the few chairs along the way. When the Reaper was within touching distance, he placed the chair on the floor close to Kali and sat down. Immediately, he removed his helmet, revealing his true self to Kali once again.

"You feeling better?" asked Andy.

Kali said nothing, partially out of the residual trauma, but mostly out of pure uncertainty of what to say.

"My doctors did their best for you," continued Andy. "I insisted on it! I wanted to make sure you were fully prepared for what's about to happen."

Still only silence from Kali, her eyes searching for some kind of context and focus.

"Oh," said Andy, "you probably have a bunch of questions going through your head right now, don't you? How am I still alive? What have I been doing? What's with the dumb costume? Et cetera! Well, here, let me give you a quick summary."

Kali's concerns secretly mounted inside her.

"So," continued Andy, "about two years ago, I got shot by my old boss, you, and left for dead! I don't quite remember the reasoning behind it—something about there needing to be 'fewer people who knew' or something like that—whatever! Anyway, instead of passively dying, I somehow survived, patched myself up, made my way back to my bike, and rode off like a bat out of hell. I ended up riding south along the coast, don't ask me why, and after a while, I guess I finally passed out! Can't imagine why.

"When I woke up again, I found myself picked up by a group of these cultists. They took me in, brought me back to health, and offered me a new shot at life. At first, I wasn't sure about the whole 'blind loyalty to Dear Leader' thing, but, after a while, I learned to fake it well enough, at least. Then I got to see how effectively their 'Dear Leader' controlled the people in this town, and, let me tell you, it was insane! Like, tin-foil-hat insane! This guy convinced these people that he could control the weather… with his feelings! Never demonstrated it, never even pretended to demonstrate it, he just said it, and that was it! How gullible can these people be, right?"

Kali's initial empathy for her former friend fell closer to the wayside as he continued his disturbing summary.

"Anyway," Andy resumed, "I decided that I needed this guy's power so I could come back to The Trade Post and get back at my old boss, you! So I spent, oh, about a year and a half playing the good little cultist, getting to work closer to 'Dear Leader' watching and observing all the patterns of his daily routine. I even learned how to imitate his voice. Then, one night, I stealthed myself into this place, made my way upstairs to his bedroom, grabbed one of the extra pillows he wasn't using, and pressed it against his surprised face until he stopped squirming!"

By this point, although Kali still had empathy for the man she had betrayed, it was hanging by a thread.

"So then," Andy blurted on, "I suddenly had this dead body on my hands! Most other people in that position would likely just panic and not think straight. But not me! I knew better! I simply took off his clothes, then removed my own, and switched our outfits! We were similar enough in build and height, thank whatever twisted god made that possible, and I was able to successfully pretend I was the same person. It's only pure luck that no one was allowed to ever see their Dear Leader's face without fear of death, but just my rotten luck that my head was just a tad smaller than his! I swear, sometimes I feel like I need some sort of super glue to make this helmet stay in place!"

At this moment, Kali wanted nothing more than to squash Andy like a bug!

"So," continued Andy, oblivious to Kali's expression of discontent, "I had to figure out what to do with the dead body. So I called for the guards and told them the dead guy tried to assassinate me. The guards took my word for it, mostly out of fear of not wanting to see my unmasked face. They actually believed I was their Dear Leader! And just like that, I became the Reaper! And here we are now, having such a nice chat!"

Kali wanted so desperately to find the right words, but none could yet reach her mind. They seemed to be hiding just around the corner.

"So," said Andy, "do you have anything you want to say to me?"

Kali's first thought was to tell Andy stop saying "so". Her second thought was a plan of escape.

Kali's eyes started to overflow with tears, accompanied by her continued silence.

Then, seemingly out of desperation, she found the words she wanted to say—the beginning of her plan.

"I'm so sorry," whispered Kali.

Andy just sat there fidgeting in his chair like a toddler fighting boredom.

"So, yeah, it's too late for that, Kali," said Andy. "If you're gonna shoot someone, you better make sure they're dead!"

Silence.

"Now," said Andy, "you were willing to kill me to keep something very important to you a secret. Whatever it is, if you're willing to go that far to keep it safe, then it must be worth a great deal. So I need you to tell me what it is and exactly where I can find it!"

Kali remained unmoved!

"I mean," continued Andy, "I have a rough idea of where it is, but I never got farther than that last time, and getting shot can mess with your memory a little bit. So are you going to tell me what I want to know, or are you going to give me the pleasure of forcing it out of you?"

Kali pretended to panic—part two of her plan.

"Okay," said Andy as he angrily got up from his chair, "I'm going back upstairs to get some of my toys. When I come back down, maybe we'll play with them, maybe we won't. Be up to you!"

As he ran up the stairs, Andy put his helmet back on, resuming the role of the Reaper. Reaching the landing, he closed and locked the door behind him.

Kali had just planted the seed; now she just had to let it grow.

# 20
# Land of the Blind

Maya, Marcus, and the other soldiers arrived at their designated base of operations with a few hours to spare before nighttime. They picked a spot on a hill with lots of tree cover, about half a mile away from the cult compound. As each soldier was preparing for their upcoming secret invasion, Marcus observed the compound and surrounding area through his old-but-powerful binoculars. As he scanned the area, a strange sense of unease came about him.

"Weird," whispered Marcus to himself.

Maya, overhearing, stepped over to Marcus to see what (if anything) was troubling him.

"What is it?" asked Maya.

Marcus continued to closely scan the area.

"This place. It seems… smaller than when I was last here."

Maya thought about that for a moment. She commented on how sometimes things can appear much bigger to us when we're kids. But Marcus had been fully grown during his time here.

"Well," said Maya, "in all honesty, it's not what I expected either!"

Based on all the rumors and vague details acquired overtime, Maya had envisioned the Dreaded Dragons compound to look more elaborate: imposing structures, lots of ruthless people, basically some kind of "evil place" from your standard fairytale. Instead, Maya and her gang were presented with what could best be described as a slightly modified suburb with a not-so-impressive-looking mansion located at the far end. Although Marcus could still make out some armed cultists, there couldn't have been more than a few dozen, tops! Almost immediately, Maya felt severely, perhaps almost comically, overprepared for this mission! Nevertheless, they had a friend to save, and in that case, more is always better!

After some final scans of the area and consulting their maps, it was decided that the best course of action was to surreptitiously move their way through the trees that ran all along the perimeter of the compound. There was also a stand of trees extending to the mansion, which provided protection from the moonlight. This would likely be the best entry point.

The only substantial challenge they faced would be navigating through the extra layer of darkness through the trees. They obviously couldn't use any torches or any other means of illumination to guide them.

"Inari can do it," said Maya.

Marcus and the others all paused what they were doing out of total befuddlement from what Maya had just said.

"No, I mean it," insisted Maya. "She's done it before. She's got great night vision! We could tie a rope to her vest and we all hold onto it while she guides us through the trees."

Although Marcus had no reason thus far to doubt Maya, or her fox companion for that matter, even this seemed far-fetched to him. But, with no other alternatives, it seemed like their best option, silly though it may have sounded to him and the others in that moment.

As Marcus continued his scanning through his binoculars, Maya took a good look at the mansion through her telescope. From her vantage point, she spotted what looked like a makeshift stage in front of the building, with pillars in a few spots and a large bell in one of the corners. *Somehow I doubt that thing is used for theater shows,* Maya thought to herself.

"That thing that looks like stage," said Marcus, "that's where the Reaper would typically host his public inquisitions, or the occasional execution."

Maya's stomach turned!

"Charming," replied Maya sarcastically. "Let's hope Kali isn't dragged up there tonight."

The group was just about ready for the mission with their weapons primed and their minds clear. By the time they reached their starting point closer to the compound, nighttime would have fallen, and they would begin their approach toward the mansion!

Meanwhile, inside the basement of the mansion, Kali was finding new ways to tolerate Andy's toys: she pretended that the burning ones felt like bug bites, that the wooden ones felt like bumping your shin into a coffee table, and the water ones felt like a gentle ocean breeze; although her game of "let's pretend" grew incrementally harder to play with the smell of blood and broken flesh perfuming the air.

"Okay," said Andy, "we've been at this for a lot longer than we should have. Clearly, I'm doing something wrong. So help me out here: what is it going to take?"

Kali looked at Andy through her swollen eye. She then took a deep and painful breath before finally speaking through her trembling lips.

"Andy," said Kali, "I made a mistake. I was a different person back then. I've already told you I was sorry, but that was clearly another mistake. I only have one more thing to say to you."

Andy leaned in and placed his hand to his ear in anticipation of what was coming.

"Go to Hell," whispered Kali.

Andy just stood there making exaggerated thinking noises as he decided what to do next.

"You know what," blurted Andy, "screw it! Whatever this thing is you're hiding, I'm sure I'll dig it up eventually. I'll just have to bring all my people with me to help find it. That'll be fun! So I'm going to go ahead and end your miserable little stinking life in the most elaborate way I can think of, just because I can. That's not unlike your rationale for shooting me!"

Andy put his helmet back on as he ascended the stairs.

"Boys," called out Andy (the Reaper), "it's time for a show!"

# 21
# For Whom the Bell Tolls

Dusk had finally settled, nighttime covered the land, and Maya's team was on the move! Maya tied a cord onto Inari's vest that stretched long enough for the whole team to latch onto. With Maya following right behind the fox, the team would make their way through the darkness of the woods with ease. What's more, Maya also knew that Inari would be able to catch Kali's scent once they were closer. They just had to hope that Kali was still there and alive.

As the team maneuvered through the trees toward the mansion, they couldn't help but notice how abnormally quiet it was this close to the town. Marcus, who'd lived there before, especially found it uncomfortably silent. It was almost like the population had suddenly evaporated. While Marcus might not go so far as to say that the compound was a veritable metropolis, at the very least, it was sufficiently populated to still have life to it, even at night. Regardless, Marcus and the others were not about to question their apparent luck at the diminished number of cultists.

Inari guided the team through the nearly impenetrable black woods, occasionally stopping to avoid obstacles ahead. At one point, Inari and the others spied a small group of cultists just on the edge of the trees nearest the compound. Everyone stopped where they were and bent down low. The cultists lingered at the same spot for quite a while before moving languidly toward another spot, allowing Inari and the others to press on.

The team was about halfway through the woods when Inari spotted a cultist about fifty feet away, inconveniently walking through the trees, directly in their path! Even in the feeble light of the waxing crescent moon, the team could see the silhouette of the cultist. They all followed Inari's lead and got down as low as they possibly could. They hoped that the cultist would eventually go back in the direction he came, but those hopes were dashed as the cultist slowly made his way closer to the team. Maya quietly drew her knife, ready to take him down if needed. The ruckus might attract other cultist guards, but it was a risk she knew she had to take.

Suddenly, the cultist stopped, fiddled with his fly, and proceeded to urinate on the nearest tree.

GONG!

The cultist was interrupted by the resonating sound of a large bell. He immediately started to sprint toward its inviting sound.

Maya looked inquisitively at Marcus.

"What the hell is that?" whispered Maya.

"Unfortunately," replied Marcus, "that's the bell from the stage in front of the mansion. That can only mean one thing!"

Maya knew just what that probably meant, and she would not allow it!

"Proceed," whispered Maya to her fox friend.

Inari continued to guide the team through the woods. Using the sound of the continuously pealing bell as cover, she could lead the team a little faster while maintaining their element of surprise.

"What are you doing?" whispered Marcus.

"We're not straying from the mission," replied Maya.

Marcus may have remained committed to rescuing Kali, but based on what that bell meant, it might already be too late.

"Listen," said Marcus, "that bell will bring the entire cult to the stage area. Even if we managed to grab Kali before, you know, we'll still be outnumbered! We won't stand a chance."

"Trust me," said Maya, "I have a nearly foolproof plan! Keep going!"

Meanwhile, in the basement of the mansion, Kali also heard the bell. She remained sitting on the edge of the cot. Even when the Reaper came back down the stairs, with the ominous clanging of the calling bell in the background, Kali didn't so much as flinch.

The Reaper kept his helmet on this time, as he was accompanied by two other cultists: one standing by at the foot of the stairs with a crossbow pistol and the other accompanying the Reaper who had been tasked with dragging Kali to her destination. The Reaper stood directly before Kali with a show of dominance, feeling overly confident in his perceived power.

"It's time for your reward and retribution," said the Reaper.

As one of the cultists unlocked Kali's ankle chain and was about to take hold of her arm, Kali decided to expend the last bit of energy she had left.

As planned, Kali channeled all of her reserved energy into her dominant hand, primed her arm, and thrust a fist of power straight at the Reaper's head, knocking his helmet clean off and revealing his face to the other cultists! The powerful blow hurt Kali more that the Reaper, excruciating pain flowed throughout Kali's body, but she didn't care. If she was marked to die, then she would die fighting!

The Reaper, seemingly oblivious to his absent helmet, looked directly at Kali with fury in his eyes.

"That's it, you little…"

Andy hesitated, suddenly aware of the cultist holding Kali in place staring at him like a frightened prey animal. Andy reflexively touched his face and realized what had happened. But before Andy could do or say anything else, a sudden burst of air whooshed past Andy's head. The next thing he knew, the cultist who had been holding Kali in place lay dead on the floor with a crossbow bolt firmly planted in his eye. Kali stood absolutely still, somewhat bewildered by what had just happened, physically unable to respond in any way.

"He saw your face," said the cultist by the stairs, "he saw your face!"

With this darkly comical situation in motion, Kali tried to make a break for it, attempting to run past Andy, but he was too quick and grabbed Kali by the arm, pulling her back and throwing her onto the cot. The momentum was enough to seriously disorient Kali for a moment.

"Bring me my helmet," ordered Andy with blood-curdling frustration in his voice.

The cultist by the stairs quickly retrieved the helmet and offered it to Dear Leader, keeping his eyes shut as he did.

Andy took his helmet and placed it back onto his undersized head.

"You may open your eyes now," said the Reaper.

The cultist did so.

"Take her," said the Reaper.

The cultist grabbed the limp and frustrated Kali. She had expended the remainder her energy, yet she still tried to fight back.

"This ends now," said the Reaper as he joined the other cultist in dragging Kali up the stairs.

Meanwhile, back in the woods, Maya and the team were closing in on the mansion. They could see the torches on the stage and the bell that was still being rung. They kept their distance from the stage, avoiding the torches. Even then, they were so close!

Suddenly, without apparent cause, Inari stopped, causing the whole chain to also stop.

"What is it?" whispered Maya.

Inari sniffed the air in all directions, trying to catch a familiar scent. Quickly, she found it and pointed her nose at the stage through the trees. Maya followed Inari's direction and was shocked to see the Reaper and another cultist dragging Kali onto the stage. Maya gestured to Marcus and the rest of the soldiers to look toward the stage.

"Dreaded Dragons," announced the Reaper, "tonight, we have found our salvation!"

The assembled cultists cheered and howled.

"For this is the woman," continued the Reaper, "who has given me the key to bring back the Days of Power!"

More cheers from the cultists.

"Liar," yelled Kali as she tried once again to struggle against the Reaper, only to be kicked back onto the floor.

Marcus gently placed his hand on Maya's shoulder as they watched the scene unfold.

"You said you had an idea," whispered Marcus. "What is it?"

"Which of your soldiers is the best marksman?" asked Maya.

The Reaper went on and on about how he made this woman reveal her secrets, how she gave him the location of their salvation, and how he would now lead them to the place promised them by his divine will! On he went, proclaiming this and that, all the while blowing hot air and not really saying much of anything—not that the cultists seemed to mind.

Meanwhile, Maya watched as one of the soldiers, the best marksman, stood by awaiting Maya's signal with her arrow primed and ready.

After a few more rounds of brashly proclaiming false prophecies, the Reaper drew his sword with one hand and pointed the blade at Kali, still lying on the floor.

"You have served your purpose," said the Reaper. "Your retribution is now at hand!"

The Reaper raised his sword, preparing to strike the greatest blow of his life!

"Now!" commanded Maya.

The soldier launched her arrow expertly at the Reaper's helmet, causing it to once again fly right off his head!

The Reaper's (Andy's) face was now visible to the entire Dreaded Dragon cult!

The cultists stood there, mystified, horrified, petrified.

Suddenly, everything went silent. Not a single bell, not a single bird, not a single voice could be heard.

Andy hesitantly lowered his sword and raised his unarmed hand to his followers.

"Okay," shouted Andy, "just wait!"

Marcus looked at Maya with some confusion.

"What the hell are you going to do?" asked Marcus.

"Just wait," replied Maya.

One of the cultists in the crowd drew his dagger and looked at the person next to him, who, in turn, drew her weapon while looking at the other cultist.

"Wait," said Andy in a calming voice.

As if they had turned deaf, all of the cultists drew their weapons.

"*Wait!*," commanded Andy.

Ignoring the command, Andy found himself witnessing his own undoing to a chorus of death! All the cultists murdered each other and themselves in a fearful frenzy—all in blind service to a single-minded fool!

Marcus and the other soldiers couldn't believe what they saw. Never had such a strange and unnerving sight brought them such horrors yet also unexpected delight.

Soon, the chorus fell silent again until there was nothing but dirt, blood, and the reflection of torch flames in fresh crimson puddles!

Andy was shaken from his shock when he heard Maya and the soldiers rushing toward the stage from the trees. In a panic, Andy hastily dropped his sword and ran directly back into the mansion.

Maya and Inari bolted toward Kali. When they were close enough, Maya held Kali in a reassuring embrace.

"Are you badly hurt?" asked Maya.

"I've been better," replied Kali.

Maya helped Kali stand up, placing one of her arms around Kali's waist. Marcus was the next one to greet her.

"Just how many lives do you have?" quipped Marcus.

Maya gently handed Kali off to Marcus.

"Here, keep her safe," said Maya. "I'm going after Andy and all of you are staying here!"

Feeling a scratch on her leg, Maya looked down at her fox friend.

"Inari, you have to stay with Kali."

With that, Maya bolted after Andy, determined to keep her rendezvous with evil!

# 22
# Here Comes a Walking Fire

As Maya made her way closer toward the mansion, she already noticed something was wrong. Through the windows, she could see fire, not just from the torches illuminating the interior but uncontained flames engulfing the insides. Andy was most likely attempting to hide his next effort to escape; *not this time*!

Maya swiftly found the entrance to the mansion and rushed straight inside. The flames had just begun to reach the entrance. Soon the entire building would be completely set ablaze. Maya suddenly saw Andy darting around the hallways with a torch, lighting up every nook and cranny.

Maya could tell that Andy had gone temporarily insane, perhaps more so than usual. With his entire cult lying dead in the courtyard and with no intel as to the whereabouts of the Machine, Andy no longer had any clear prospects to speak of. Yet his desperate effort to cling to even a shred of his former power drove him to this final act of madness, burning away his failure with ambitions to rise from the ashes.

In that moment, Maya knew exactly what to do.

Suddenly, Andy dropped his torch onto the floor and bolted toward the back of the mansion. Maya gave chase and followed Andy through the burning hallway to the back door, leading to the large rear deck. The flames had not yet reached this part of the house but they were quickly finding their way over. Andy was just about to make his escape through a small gate that lead to a flight of stairs toward the woods.

"Andy," called out Maya.

Her shout went ignored.

"I have what you're looking for," she said. "I know where it is!"

Andy stopped his frantic escape and stared at Maya like a starving man being offered a meaty bone.

"Tell me," demanded Andy.

Maya drew her knife and took on a fighting stance.

"Make me," retorted Maya tauntingly.

Andy drew his large dagger and charged toward Maya.

Maya's martial arts training kicked in as she used Andy's forward momentum to redirect him into an old deck chair, causing him to tumble over and fumble. Andy quickly regained his balance and prepared for a serious fight, having, in that moment, gained a better understanding what kind of fighter Maya was.

During this brief standoff, Maya suddenly had a few flashes of memories from two years ago. She couldn't help but notice how this fight was incredibly similar to the one she had against her opponent's friend: the fire, the knives, and especially the hatred radiating toward her. As she noticed the parallels, she wondered if history would repeat itself. Surely, she was counting on it!

The fight continued inconclusively—slashing and clashing with strikes that always seemed to get close but without impact, all the while the nearby mansion became more and more of an inferno; the flames inching their way onto the deck, with sparks reaching some of the nearby furniture setting them ablaze.

"What is this thing that's so important to you, huh?!" shrieked Andy.

"You didn't deserve to know," replied Maya, "not now, not ever!"

Andy let out a few angry and profane grunts in frustration.

"Just give up, Andy," said Maya. "It's all over! Your cult is dead, and even if you learn where it is, you'll never be able to use it!"

"Don't be so sure of that, kid," responded Andy, whose mind was calming down. "This world is chalk full of all kinds of gullible dolts just waiting for someone to take control of their lives."

"You mean brainwash," Maya contradicted.

"Call it what you want," said Andy. "It's just human stupidity to me!"

Andy moved in for another attack. Maya made a different move to avoid getting hit, but her timing was off by a split second, causing her to get a minor slash on her upper arm.

As Andy looked back and saw what he had done, he observed the blood on his dagger before grinning at Maya.

"First blood," said Andy. "It would seem this fight favors me!"

Maya ignored the taunt.

"Why do you even bother protecting this thing whatever it is?" asked Andy. "If it's really that big of a deal, someone will find it eventually. So it might as well be me!"

"Not while I live," said Maya.

A dark grin slashed across Andy's face.

"I can fix that!"

The fight grew more intense, the nearby flames grew radically higher, and the fighters' wills grew exponentially stronger!

Finally the tables turned when Andy managed to sneak in a strike on Maya's leg, jamming the dagger deeply into her left thigh. Maya tumbled onto the floor, dropping her knife and watched it slide a few yards away. Realizing his advantage, Andy leapt on top of Maya, pinning her down and pressing his knee against her injured leg. Maya fought back but his weight was too much.

"I don't need you to tell me anything anyway," said Andy. "Like I told Kali, I'll just look harder!"

Andy wrapped his hands around Maya's throat and squeezed. Maya gasped for air, tried to reach for Andy's face to shove a finger into his eye, but it was just out of reach.

"I'll kill you," said Andy, "then I'll go back to your tiny village and kill every single person in that little house of yours before I burn it down, along with everything there. Then, I'll start my search for whatever it is you're hiding, and…"

Before Andy could finish that thought, Maya yanked the dagger out of her leg and jammed it into Andy's right side, causing him to loose his grip on Maya's neck and allowing her to breath again. Andy fell off of Maya, screaming in agony.

Maya awkwardly rolled over and started to crawl away, trying to retrieve her own knife as she struggled for breath.

Andy had pulled the dagger out of his side. As he stood up, he grabbed an old rocking chair, half lit on fire, and stumbled toward Maya who was still struggling to reach her knife.

Just when Maya's blade was within arm's reach, Andy raised the flaming chair over his head. His eyes gleamed just as fiery as the mansion itself, ready to slam the chair onto Maya's head.

Suddenly, Andy was hit by a massive pain in his groin. Inari had leapt into the fray and was crushing Andy's genitalia with her jaws. Andy dropped the flaming chair to the side and was about to try and grab the fox. Just before Andy could get a grip on the red creature, Inari jumped away and landed directly on top of Maya's back, as if trying to keep her low to the ground for some reason.

As Andy stood there in complete agony, he suddenly looked up and saw a haunting sight. Before him, outlined by the flames, was Kali, six-shooter in hand, aimed directly at Andy once again.

"No," said Andy.

Without warning, Kali fired a single shot, hitting Andy's chest and exiting through his back. Then, in rapid fire, another, and another, and another, and another, and another! All six shots went clean through Andy's body as he tumbled over and fell backwards.

Kali stood over Andy's punctured body and watched. Andy looked back up at Kali with fury, confusion, and frustration in his eyes.

"Not this time, Andy," said Kali.

Then, there came one final breath from Andy, until he was unquestionably gone!

Kali immediately lent her attention to Maya and Inari. The fox, knowing the situation was considerably improved, lifted herself up from Maya. Nudging her face against Maya's hand, Inari slid her body under Maya's arm. Maya, in turn, grabbed the handle affixed to Inari's vest as she lifted herself up. Inari guided the two women away from the fire and to safety, leaving Andy's lifeless body to burn.

Marcus and the others waited outside for any sign of their sisters-in-arms. Suddenly, there they were, silhouetted by the now fully-flaming mansion. Marcus and the others ran over to the trio and helped them move away from the flames.

"I owe you twice now," said Maya, "right?"

"Tell you what," said Kali, "we'll call it even."

Maya and Kali smiled at each other as Inari remained by their sides, admiring the light shinning between them both.

# 23
# Getting Better

Within a few days of their victory against the Dreaded Dragons, Maya and the rest of the gang made their way back to The Trade Post. Kali and Maya immediately sent themselves to the infirmary. Kali was undergoing treatments for multiple injuries and was expected to make a substantially full recovery. Meanwhile, Maya had her stab wound treated and would have to walk around with a cane for a little while, but she would also live. Inari may not have had any injuries to speak of, but at Maya's insistence, she was rewarded for her efforts with a luxurious bath, followed by a hearty meal consisting mostly of her favorite chicken skewers.

Maya decided to wait for her leg wound to sufficiently heal before heading home, so she and Inari had some spare time to enjoy.

Maya's first order of business during her recovery was to present Marcus with a special gift, which arrived at The Trade Post shortly before they did. Maya knocked on Marcus' door and waited. When Marcus answered, he was greeted by Maya and… some other girl?

Accompanying Maya was a young woman named Ruth—a shorter girl with curly, dark hair, hazel eyes, and a cheerful smile. She was also covered with elegant tattoos and a few piercings here and there.

"Hi there. I'm Ruth. Nice to meet you," she said, offering her hand to Marcus.

"Uh, hello," said Marcus, taking the girl's hand. "What's this all about?"

"Oh, Ruth here was just telling me," said Maya, "about her hobby as a tattoo artist and how she specializes in alterations."

"Yup," replied Ruth, "I came all the way from Ashland. My friend Michael, you've met him, said that Maya wanted to invite me here to change up your ink. Is that true?"

Marcus looked at Maya with a profound sense of warm admiration before answering Ruth.

"Yes," said Marcus, "that's true."

"Okay, then," cheered Ruth, "let's get to work!"

Ruth entered Marcus' home with her tattoo kit in hand. She had learned the more ancient techniques for tattooing and also had a reputation for possessing a gentle touch, even on the more elaborate works of body art she had done. Ruth took a long look at Marcus' original tattoo and drew her new custom design on some parchment. Once satisfied with the concept, Ruth took out the needles and ink and got to work, applying many shades of blue to and around the black dragon on Marcus' shoulder.

"So," said Ruth, "what are you trying to make better?"

Marcus looked directly at Maya with a smile and then at Ruth.

"Everything," said Marcus.

"Hey," said Ruth to Maya, "you want something for yourself while I'm here?"

"Oh, no thanks," responded Maya. "I'm good right now."

"Okay," said Ruth. "I'm just saying, you've got the skin for some ink."

Maya chuckled.

"Maybe in the future," said Maya.

After a little over two hours, Ruth had finished her latest masterpiece. The dark and angry dragon had been transformed into a tranquil water dragon, ocean waves splashing and flowing every which way in elegant patterns. Underneath the waves were the words, "Destination: Unknown." Marcus took a long look at the new ink in the mirror and was stunned to feel so different, so much better than ever before. He was amazed at how something so simple could have such an impact on one's perception.

Ruth gave Marcus some aftercare instructions along with a few jars of miscellaneous homemade skin treatments. Once her work was complete, Ruth politely excused herself and left. Maya was just about on her way out the door as well, when…

"Wait," said Marcus. "I have something for you, too."

Marcus retreated to his bedroom for a moment and then returned with a small, metallic box lined with silk and deeply rusted on the hinge. As Maya opened the box, she was greeted by a stunning sight: a centuries-old, well-polished Distinguished Service Medal of the U.S. Coast Guard.

"It was my grandmother's," said Marcus. "I think it should belong to you now. I still have yet to feel that I'm worthy of keeping it."

"Well," said Maya, "tell you what. I'll serve as this medal's guardian until you do feel worthy. Sound good?"

Marcus smiled.

"Indeed!"

"Thank you," said Maya with a returning smile.

After that, Maya made her way to the infirmary to check in on Kali. She was still a bit weak from her ordeal, but she was strong and would pull through like she always did; at least, that's what she kept telling Maya. While Maya had no doubt of her friend's resolve and determination, Maya still insisted that Kali listen to the doctors—a suggestion that may have frustrated Kali a bit, but she tended to take her friend's words to heart. After a few more laughs and some pleasant conversation, Maya told Kali that she would be heading home in the morning. She felt well enough to drive again and needed to continue her efforts to better prepare Douglass Ranch for future situations like it had recently experienced.

"Don't be a stranger, Maya," said Kali as she rested.

"Never," replied Maya.

After a full night's rest, followed by a hearty breakfast, Maya and Inari packed up and were ready to head for home. Kali and

Marcus both greeted them at the gate to bid them a fond farewell. Maya and Inari both said their goodbyes, mounted the Beast, and rode off into the shining morning light.

# Epilogue

FOR MAYA'S AND KALI'S
EYES ONLY

Winter, 2086

My dear Maya,

At the time of my typing this letter, your friend, Lylla, will have left here for her home after bringing you back to us. I am grateful to know you have made so many wonderful friends like Lylla in your travels.

Oh, wait, I meant to call her by her real name, Kali.

Yes, my dear, I knew exactly who she was! I'm not entirely sure why you felt the need to keep it a secret from me, but I can venture a few guesses. Needless to say, whatever your reasonings, I understand. It seems only fair that you be allowed to have secrets of your own after dealing with what I had kept from you for so long: hiding my knowledge of The Wave. I know we made our peace with all that, but I still cannot say enough just how sorry I am and how much your forgiveness means to me.

Earlier this morning I had a delightful conversation with Kali. It seems that neither of us could get any sleep that night, as though we both needed to confront our demons, as they say. You will be happy to hear that Kali and I have made our peace with each other. I hope to see her again soon in the future.

I don't know what agreement you made with her regarding the Machine, but I have full confidence in your joint efforts to prepare for a better future: both for yourselves and for those who will come after.

I do not intend to leave this world after writing this letter to you both, but should that come to pass, know that I will always be with you both in spirit and that I will have passed contently and wholeheartedly proud of you both. I know your future will be grander than anyone could have ever imagined, and I will gladly watch it unfold from wherever I may be.


May your lights always shine, my dears!

Dougie

That letter had been written five months ago. Maya and Kali had only now read it together for the first time. Maya found it in Dougie's desk when she was writing invitations for her messenger ravens. Maya waited until Kali had arrived before breaking the seal, and they were both glad she did.

After reading the letter together, Maya placed it back inside its original envelope and put it in her pocket.

"You okay?" asked Kali.

"I'll be fine," replied Maya with a tear forming in her eye.

Kali embraced her friend, as did Inari in her own way.

"You ready?" asked Kali.

Maya looked down at her fox companion, who appeared calm and alert.

"I think so," replied Maya.

With that, Maya, Inari, and Kali walked out of the house together and down the pathway toward the center of the village.

The main tent had been temporarily taken down, the pillars covered with salvaged flame-retardant fabric, and all the picnic tables moved away. In the center was a large and delicately structured funeral pyre, decorated with flowers and wreaths; and in the center rested Dougie's body on a wooden platform.

The pyre was surrounded by the gathered population of Douglass Ranch, along with nearby villagers who knew Dougie well, like Michael and little Izzy. Also attending were Marcus and his fellow soldiers, who had come to mourn with their sisters-in-arms.

A moment of silence lingered before Maya spoke.

"My great aunt," said Maya, "was one of the most resilient and compassionate people I have ever known. I am grateful for the time I had with her, as I'm sure all of you are as well. But, let us not mourn this day. Instead, let us celebrate the memories we all made with her—the ones we will share with our loved ones and them with theirs."

"In that way," continued Maya, "she will never be gone; rather, she will always be with us!"

With that, Maya removed the letter from her pocket and placed it on top of Dougie's peaceful body, weighing it down with a small, smooth stone. Kali placed her hand on top of Maya's as she rested the paper down. The two women shared a reassuring glance of sisterhood, finalizing a bond that would not be easily broken.

As the two women kept their hands quietly on Dougie's body for just a moment, Inari let out several mournful cries, almost howls, saying goodbye in her own way, before backing away from the pyre.

Still joining hands, Maya and Kali stepped away as Maya was presented with a torch from her blacksmith friend, Joseph. Maya gazed at Dougie's face one last time.

"Goodbye, Dougie," whispered Maya. "I love you."

And with that, Maya thrust the torch into the pyre. Everyone watched in silence as the thrusting flames rose above their heads, solidifying Dougie's new relationship with the world.

Maya and Kali held onto each others hands for as long as they watched the flames. Inari remained close by her best friend, resting her head against Maya's leg, the flames reflecting in her dual-colored eyes.

A moment later, Michael broke the silence and brought everyone together in unison with a song penned by the late classical poet, Alfred, Lord Tennyson:

> For tho' from out our bourne of
> Time and Place
> The flood may bear me far,
> I hope to see my Pilot face to face
> When I have cross'd the bar.

THE END

# Appendix

Cults and their Followers - p.327

Original Poetry - p.333

# *Cults and Their Followers*
## Excerpt from the memoirs of Marcus Goldman

In modern Western cultures, the word "cult" is associated most frequently with unorthodox, devil worshiping, fanatic, crazy people. But in the rest of the world and throughout most of history, a cult is and was viewed as simply another form of belief, another way of understanding where we came from and why…and where are we going.

The answer you will receive from a person randomly selected from the face of this planet to the question "What is a cult?" will be as varied as that same random person's response to "What is normally served at dinner in your home?" In short, what a cult is depends entirely on where and when you find yourself.

The two most frequent definitions of "cult" in the Western World are:

1. A quasi-religious organization using devious psychological techniques to gain control over the minds and actions of adherents.

2. A group bound together tightly by an exclusive ideology and ritual practices centered on sacred symbols with an intense devotion to a specific person, idea, or activity.

A more global and thus, I believe, more accurate and useful definition is:

A cult is built around an idea (any idea) where the idea is passionately (not intellectually) known by the cultists to be the Absolute Truth, Never to Be Questioned, requiring Absolute Obedience. The Idea (whatever it is) justifies the total obliteration of the existing order because the Idea is perfection and purity…regardless of how cruelly it is applied to the world and regardless of how destructive that application may appear to be.

In 1951, the social philosopher Eric Hoffer wrote the definitive book on this topic, *The True Believer, Thoughts on the Nature of Mass Movements.* After settling at The Trade Post, I was fortunate enough to find a copy of this book. That book has resided in the bookstand next to my bed wherever that has been located ever since. It's still worth a read today.

The important point to always place front and center in your mind when thinking about or analyzing cults and cultist behavior is that it does not matter what the specific idea in question may be. It could be that the Idea is that The Meaning of Life is inscribed in an alien language on a golden obelisk located on the far side of a planet far, far away and understood only by the cult's leader (who is always given a magnificent title, such as Vanguard, Savior, Dear Leader, The Eternal One, etc.).

It is equally important to keep in mind that an Idea that is today's cult may become tomorrow's absolutely ordinary and customary basis for cultural propriety. For example, early Christianity was considered to be a wild and dangerous cult, its members to be killed or imprisoned and the Idea suppressed…until Emperor Constatine decided that it was The Idea of the Day and all the other myriad and accepted belief systems prevalent in Ancient Rome became prohibited cults.

To best comprehend what a cult is, think of cults as metaphoric fashion fads… hemlines rise and fall; specific colors blaze and fade; materials may be woven, knitted, glued, cut from whole hides, extracted from birds or reptiles or fish, or even extruded from plastic molds. These alterations are always under the absolute control of the Fashion God of the Moment (e.g., Armani, de la Renta, Dior, Saint Laurent…and earlier such distant designer deities as Worth, Poiret, and Lady Gordon). The important aspect always is that the Idea shaping the fashion-of-the-moment or the cult-of-the-moment is eternally correct and gloriously immutable…no matter how much the original Idea is altered, mutilated, or reinterpreted by the Great Leader.

The fashion fad metaphor also assists in understanding why cult members are so fanatically loyal to the Idea and to the Dear Leader. People slavishly follow both the rules of fashion and the rules of the cult because they demonstrate one or more (usually many more) of the following characteristics:

- Insecurity
- Having extremely low self-esteem (e.g., hate themselves for some reason)
- Fear
- Confusion
- Anger/Disappointment
- Too uneducated to think for themselves
- Too brain lazy to think for themselves
- Too undernourished to think for themselves
- So totally brainwashed in their youth that they can't conceive of anything other than the Idea. This last characteristic is the most insidious of them all by far. By way of a fashion example, how many boys would

willingly wear a dress to the school dance? By way of a cult example, how many Roman citizens attempted to save otherwise innocent and innocuous Christians from being sacrificed in the arena?

Cult followers will do anything to please the Dear Leader, no matter how abhorrent or even self-destructive the commanded action may be. Why? Because the follower's entire being is subsumed in the Idea. Fulfilling the wishes of the Dear Leader is not optional.

What makes any cultist so dangerous is that they operate without any thought of the consequences of their actions. In the Days of Power, and in some parts of the world today, most people have been raised by overindulgent parents in a fantasy world without adverse consequences, the destructive potential and power of cultism are even more pernicious.

# Original Poetry By Zack Gibson

<u>Green Torches</u>
Green
Eyes that Perceive
Torches we light
Sacrifice to preserve

<u>Poor Leadership</u>
Arrogance is not a justification for ignorance, it's the excuse of those without merit dipped in a fondue of blindness

<u>Time Is Not Wasted</u>
Days gone are not days lost, the only day is today

<u>The Beast</u>
Rubber spheres grind dirt to propel us forward
Fellowship through riding these deserted lands

As time becomes more and more
subjective to those who are
truly free

### Inari's Wisdom
Innocence is preserved through
the compassion of a fox
Magic within the fabrics of
the branches that support us

### Disarmed
The loss of a friend is like
the loss of an arm, it's hard
to grasp reality with one
grip

### Pressure
The past does not weigh as
much to those who haven't
experienced it directly
Though the scars of the past
are seen on their skin

### Weasels
There is no more deadly of a
weapon than a shared secret

### Legacy of Gaia
Attach not to me, but my
memory

As my ideas are meant to stay
as I am meant to fade
All teachings resurrect those
who lay in the grave


<u>Be Wary of Sheep</u>
One sheep is dinner
Two sheep for a tailor
Three sheep to start a savior
A herd of sheep stays flocked
forever

<u>Lethal Treasure Hunt</u>
If the pursuit of the hidden
costs of our lives, is it
worth finding in the end?

<u>Trespasser</u>
You cannot own a space that
you are a guest in
Appreciate what you have
rather than focus on what you
can take
Power comes from respect, not
fear

www.ingramcontent.com/pod-product-compliance
Lightning Source LLC
LaVergne TN
LVHW011944060526
838201LV00061B/4202